"Not that the story need be long, but it will take a long while to make it short."

— Henry David Thoreau

The Moccasin Telegraph and Other Stories

W.P. Kinsella was born in 1935 in Edmonton, Alberta. This is his fourth collection of stories set on the Hobbema Reserve. His stories have been widely published in Canadian and American magazines and have appeared in many anthologies including *Pushcart Prize V (1980-81), Best Canadian Short Stories* and *The Penguin Book of Modern Canadian Short Stories.*

In 1982 his novel, *Shoeless Joe,* was published to great acclaim, winning the Houghton Mifflin Literary Fellowship Award.

THE MOCCASIN TELEGRAPH

and other stories

by W.P. KINSELLA

Penguin Books

Penguin Books Ltd., Harmondsworth, Middlesex, England
Penguin Books, 40 West 23rd Street, New York, New York, 10010,
U.S.A.
Penguin Books Australia Ltd., Ringwood, Victoria, Australia
Penguin Books Canada Ltd., 2801 John Street, Markham,
Ontario, Canada L3R 1B4
Penguin Books (N.Z.) Ltd., 182-190 Wairau Road, Auckland 10,
New Zealand

Published in 1983
Reprinted 1984 (twice)

*All the characters in this book are fictitious, and any
resemblance to actual persons living or dead is coincidental.*

Canadian Cataloguing in Publication Data

Kinsella. W. P.
   The moccasin telegraph and other stories

ISBN 0-14-006772-8

I. Title.

PS8571.I57M67   C813'.54   C83-098085-7
PR9199.3.K59M62

Book Design by Anodos Studios/Pamela Patrick.
Manufactured in Canada by Webcom Limited

For my daughter Lyndsey

THE BOTTLE QUEEN was a winner of The Okanogan Short Fiction Award and was published in *Canadian Author and Bookman*.

STRINGS appeared in *Release*.

THE MOCCASIN TELEGRAPH appeared in *Aquarius*.

GREEN CANDLES appeared in *The Journal of Canadian Fiction* under the title FATA MORGANA.

THE SENSE SHE WAS BORN WITH appeared in *Matrix*.

THE BALLAD OF THE PUBLIC TRUSTEE was published by *Matrix* and later appeared as a chapbook published by William Hoffer Standard Editions, Vancouver, B.C.

DR. DON has been accepted for publication by *Heartland*.

NESTS has been accepted for publication by *The Iowa Review*.

VOWS appeared in *Interface*.

THE QUEEN'S HAT was published by *Canadian Forum*.

PIUS BLINDMAN IS COMING HOME appeared in *The Western Producer*.

CONTENTS

THE BOTTLE
QUEEN

WHEN I WAS just a kid, my father, Paul Ermineskin, took off for the city, and I only seen him a few times in the last ten years. He hang around the bars and missions in the city and last time I seen him he was in bad shape and I didn't figure he had long left to live. So it sure is a surprise when he come walking into the Hobbema Pool Hall one afternoon.

"Hey, Silas," he say to me, and give my hand a shake. There is something sneaky about Pa, maybe it is the way he walks kind of sideways, with his eyes always darting all over the place. The weather is cold and it due to snow any minute but Pa is wearing only a red-silk western shirt, have black fringes all down the sleeves, and pants look like they come from a businessman's suit.

He buys a round of pop and Frito chips for me and my friends, tells us stories that make us laugh and shows us a new way to play 8-Ball that we never seen before. Pa smells of whisky, but he ain't drunk; in fact he looks healthier than I ever remember seeing him.

"You know I sure would like to see the other kids, Silas," he say to me. "I wonder if you might sort of ask your Ma if it would be okay?"

1

Pa smile at me when he say that and I can see that him and me look quite a lot alike. I frown some. Me and Ma and all the kids but Delores got more than our share of bad memories about Pa. Delores, she wasn't even born yet, though Ma's belly was big with her, when Pa left for good.

"Hey, Silas, look at me," says Pa. "You ever seen me lookin' so good? I straightened myself out some. Been off the booze and eatin' good meals. Even got a job lined up." He smile again and slap me on the arm.

"A guy who's able to charm the warts off a toad," is how Mad Etta, our medicine lady, describe Paul Ermineskin.

"Hmmfff," Ma say when I tell her Pa is back on the reserve. "He better not come around when he's drunk, if he know what's good for him." Then when I mention he want to see the kids, "They're all big enough to make their own minds up," she says. "Just let me know so's I can be away if he comes around."

Of the kids, only Delores is interested. Thomas, and Hiram, and Minnie, young as they were, all have enough bad thoughts about Pa not to want to see him.

Pa stay with an old friend of his, Isaac Hide. He keep asking me for my sister Illianna's address in Calgary but I keep pretending I forgot to look it up. Illianna is married to a white man, live in a big, new house. Pa wouldn't be comfortable there.

Delores has never had a father, and I guess has always wished for one. She keep a picture of Jay Silverheels the movie actor, and Allen Sapp the artist, pinned to the wall, and I heard her tell a girlfriend once that the picture of Allen Sapp was really one of her father.

Pa and me was still a hundred yards from the cabin when Delores explode out the door and hang herself on his neck. If you want to see somebody get hugged, you look at Paul Ermineskin that afternoon. Delores glue herself to his hand and lead him around the reserve like he never been here before. She tell him all about how she is the best bottle collector there is, and show him the forty or so dozen beer bottles stacked by the side of the cabin.

Ordinarily, bottles left around like that would disappear real quick, but me and my friends Frank Fence-post and Rufus Firstrider let it be known anybody stealing from Delores have to deal with us. The younger kids is enough afraid, especially of Frank who like to act tough, that they leave things be.

People who know her, call Delores *The Bottle Queen*. That is because she is able to collect more beer bottles and pop bottles than anybody around the reserve.

"If you throw a bottle out the door of your cabin, Delores Ermineskin will catch it before it hits the ground," Mad Etta say of her, and she say it with a prideful smile.

Delores take dancing lessons from Molly Thunder and Carson Longhorn. They is about the best chicken dancers around. Twice a week, Delores pack up her costume what Ma made out of an old dress, stuff it in a shopping bag comes from the Shoppers Drug Mart in Wetaskiwin, and head down to Blue Quills Hall for her lesson.

Carson Longhorn tell me she is really good. She win the prize for Girls Under 12 at our own pow-wow, and she win again, a five dollar prize, at the Rocky Mountain House rodeo. "If she had the money to travel to more pow-wows, she'd win almost every time," Carson tell me.

Delores is sometimes shy and sometimes bold. She can be as determined as a bird pulling a worm out of the ground. Her eyes is black and move fast as a crow's. She can spot a bottle in a ditch from a hundred yards. Sometimes when we drive back from Wetaskiwin or Ponoka, even at night, she spot a glint in the ditch, no more of a shine than a firefly, and she make me stop the truck. I watch her disappear into the ditch, walking real determined, hiking up her jeans, her pigtails what by that time of day coming undone, bouncing on her shoulders in the glow from the truck lights. In a minute she come back, usually with a bottle in each hand, grinning like somebody just give her a dollar. In winter, she can tell whether a hole in a snow drift been made by wind, an animal, or a bottle. She wade right in, have almost to swim against the drifts sometimes, but she come out grip a bottle in her mitten, have snow on her clothes right up to the armpit.

Delores have a reason for collecting all the bottles she does. Molly Thunder, her dance teacher, also make costumes. Boy, at the pow-wows you see some dancers decked up in costumes make them look like a rainbow when they twirl around as they dance. Molly make those kind, fancy ones with real coloured feathers in the bustle and headdress, and the jackets and moccasins she makes be solid beadwork done on real buckskin. Molly sell them costumes for sometimes a thousand dollars and Indian dancers from all over Canada order their dancing dress from her.

Molly promise to sell Delores a costume at cost for only $300. "A champion dancer should have fancy duds," is what Molly says, and Delores she look at them costumes, finger the beadwork and feathers every time she at Molly's cabin.

"How can somebody who's only ten years old earn three hundred dollars?" Delores ask me. I suggest she collect bottles, but I thought she'd get tired of it in a few days, like kids do, not that she'd take her collecting serious as a religion. Every day after school she go off with her gunnysack dragging behind her and walk the ditches of Highway 2A either south or north from Hobbema. She also stay up late on weekend nights when people are partying and circulate from cabin to cabin. "Soon as an empty or nearly empty bottle been set down on a table it disappear under Delores' coat," people say.

But they don't say it mean. Everybody is kind of proud to see a young girl work as hard as she does.

Sometimes Delores is like a growed up woman, especially when she is working, or counting her money which she collect in one dollar bills, "'Cause I look like I'm more rich that way." Other times when she smile up at me showing how one of her big front teeth is only half-way grown in, she is like a little girl.

She is like a little girl with Pa. If being loved could make you a better person then Pa would be about equal to an angel. And Pa, I guess is affected some by the way she treat him. One day after him and Isaac Hide been to town drinking he give to Delores a barrette for her hair. It not an ordinary one, but is made from leather with pretty beads all over it. "This here belong to your Grandma Ermineskin," I hear him tell Delores. "She used to dance in all the pow-wows and was as good as anybody. Guess you take after her."

Well, Delores couldn't of liked that barrette better if it was made of solid diamonds. She don't wear it in her hair but carry it on a thick string around her neck and show it to anybody she meet, whether they interested or not.

It make me mad to see Pa do that to her. It is the first I ever heard of my grandma being a dancer, though she did die before I was born and I don't know too much about her. But the idea of Pa carrying anything around with him for more than a month or so is not very likely. Pa, he don't own nothing but the clothes on his back, and when he's drunk I think he even sometimes lose some of them.

Him and Isaac Hide drink a lot at the Alice Hotel beer parlour the last couple of weeks and Pa look like he going back to his habit of not eating very often.

One afternoon when we hanging around the Hobbema Pool Hall, Bert Cardinal get off the southbound bus. Bert he been in jail for a few months for driving off with a car don't belong to him. "Hey, Paul, what you up to since you got out?" is the first thing he say to my papa.

Pa try to pretend like he don't hear the question, but Bert carry right on in a loud voice. "They had to throw Paul here out; he liked Fort Saskatchewan Jail so much he wanted to stay there permanent," and he slap Pa on the back.

So now I know why he ain't been drinking for a year and been eating good. "Hey, Silas," Bert says, "you should of seen your old man the day he got busted. Was walking out of Woodward's with a chainsaw in each hand. They give him eighteen months but they throw him out in twelve."

I look at Pa. "I never lied to you," he says, "you just never asked." But he got a foxy look about him anyway.

Quite a few times I take Delores out in Louis Coyote's pickup truck, look for bottles. I stop on the shoulder of the road let Delores out, and she head off down the ditch in kind of a zig-zag run. I drive ahead exactly a mile, stop and walk the ditch ahead, putting bottles in the gunny-sack I'm dragging along. I'd only get a half-mile or so down the road when the truck catch up with me. I can see Delores kneeling on the front seat, grinning and steering as the truck bump down the shoulder. When she want to stop, she disappear from sight and I know she pressing with all her might on both the clutch and the brake.

One time I even complained to her about all the bottles she was collecting. "You know me and Frank used to gather up bottles to buy gas for the truck," I said. "Now there ain't a bottle in all of Hobbema for us to find." I was sorry right away that I said it, but me and Frank wanted to take our girls for a ride, and we was broke.

"You and Frank don't collect bottles, you steal them," said Delores.

"Sometime Frank he borrow a case or two from some-body's yard..."

"Frank steals," said Delores, sounding like a nun or a school teacher.

After supper that night Delores come into our cabin with four cases of beer bottles stacked in her arms like cord-wood. I couldn't even see her face behind them.

"I'm sorry, Silas," she said. "These will give you enough gas money to get to town and back," and she set the bottles on the table and lean in and kiss my cheek. Of course I didn't take them, even though I really would of liked to.

One afternoon in the pool hall Pa he is bragging about how him and Isaac Hide going into business together, when I hit him up about giving that barrette to Delores. I checked with Ma and Mad Etta and they say Grandma Ermineskin, though she could build a teepee and run a cross-cut saw like a man, was never one to dance. "Why'd you tell Delores that?" I ask. "You know she gonna find you out for a liar." I notice Pa is still wearing that red shirt with the fringes; the silky material got a fine glaze of dirt over it now. "Hey, who's gonna tell her?" say Pa, "you?"

"It don't be long until Delores recognize that barrette as something come from a craft-store in Wetaskiwin," I say.

"She's just a little girl," says Pa. "Leave her be." And he look mean at me out of his bloodshot eyes.

Next afternoon Delores talk me into driving her and her bottles into Wetaskiwin to the bottle depot. An old man in a dirty parka and a long-billed red cap tote up her take, which come to $49 and she take it all in ones as usual.

"Only thirty more dollars and I got enough for my costume," she announce as we driving back. I try to talk her into spend a dollar or two for some burgers and Cokes but she won't do it.

We return Louis Coyote's truck to him and walk back to our cabin. Soon as we walk into the cabin I know something is wrong. There is a rustling noise from Delores' and Minnie's room, which is marked off by a sheet been throwed over some clothes-line cord.

When I move aside the sheet there is Paul Ermineskin, on his hands and knees, busy stuffing money into his pockets. Delores she keep her costume money stashed safe in a Kellogg's Corn Flake box, under some clothes on the floor of her room.

"What are you doing?" I yell, though there is no need to ask.

Pa look up and make kind of sick smile. "Hey, I was just counting the money for the kid, ya know."

If I looked at him any meaner he'd be deep-fried.

"I thought you was low-down the last time I seen you," I say.

"Hey, I was gonna pay her back..."

Delores has followed me across the cabin and now she hangs on to my arm, real tight, and sniffles some. She looks at Pa, her eyes wide, not understanding. "All you had to do was ask," she say in a small, tear-choked voice.

"I was doing it for you," Pa says to Delores. "This other guy and me we going to go out and cut Christmas trees. We got a chance to make a lot of money..." and his voice kind of trail off. The money is laying there all mixed in with Delores' clothes. Pa takes some dollars from his shirt pocket and throws them down.

"Well, I better get going," Pa says, standing up, "got to head for Edmonton, find my partner and get to work." He push past me and head for the door.

"No," says Delores, "don't go yet." She let go of my arm, run over scoop up some money and hold it out to Pa, who has stopped and turned around.

Pa flash a smile at her, like a weasel just been invited into a hen house.

"You don't want to give him nothing, Delores," I say.

"Yes, I do," she say, real final like.

"You know I'm gonna pay you back," says Pa, smiling again.

I got my fists clenched, and even though I hardly ever raise up my hand against anybody, right now I'd like to punch that smile right through to the back of his neck.

"Just go," says Delores, pushing more money at Pa who is stuffing it in all his pockets, even pushing some down the neck of his shirt what don't have no buttons on the front. When Pa got the money all stashed he wheel around and skulk out the door, giving us a little wave over his shoulder.

When we can't hear his boots on the snow no more, Delores rush over and throw her arms around me and hug real hard. She sob loud into my chest.

Maybe she have just the slightest suspicion he was telling the truth. After a while her crying slow down some. I tip her head up so I can see her face, and kiss her forehead. She looks so much like Pa. Maybe that was it, maybe she can feel his blood travelling around in her.

She is wearing that beaded barrette Pa gave her, not in her hair, but hanging from around her neck, it rest in a spot where she gonna grow breasts in a couple of years.

Still sniffling, she undo the barrette and hold it in the palm of her hand.

"Did this really belong to my Grandma Ermineskin, Silas?" she say to me, looking me right in the face with her wet, black eyes.

This is sure my chance to tan Paul Ermineskin's hide. And I'm mad enough to do it. But when I look at Delores it seem to me she lost enough already today. I can't believe she doesn't know the truth. I think the woman in her does, but it is the little girl who is asking the question. And if she has to ask I know what answer she want to hear.

STRINGS

I WAS SITTING in the sun on a turned-over washtub when Ellsworth come walking by my cabin. He got his hands in the pockets of his heavy denim and buckskin jacket and he have the woolly collar turned up against the frosty fall air. I just know him to see him. We never talked to each other and I only heard about the trouble he is in.

"You're Silas?" he say to me. He rock back on his heels, his hands still in his pockets.

"Yeah," I say, trying to decide what it is he might want with me.

"I'm Ellsworth Shot-both-sides," he say, be quiet for a second, then add, "I suppose you heard of me?"

"I know your name."

"Everybody do. You just have to kill somebody to get everybody to know you." And he smile at me from his long oval face. He have his hair in two braids to his shoulders and his nose be long and straight. He got a lean look about him, like a starved dog.

"What can I do for you?" I say.

"I read your book. My cousin give it to me. I liked it...and I was wondering..." He reach inside his jacket

11

and bring out a few sheets of folded yellow paper and hand them to me. Then he turn around and walk away.

"I'll come back in a day or two," he say over his shoulder.

Ellsworth been down on his luck of late. About four months ago he got charged with a murder. Happened at a drunk-up way back on the reserve. He shot a guy named Joey Owl. His Legal Aid lawyer somehow got him out on bail, I don't understand how things like that work, and he is sort of free until his trial come up in the winter.

I heard too that his wife left him and took their kids.

What he's given me is kind of a diary written on pages been torn from a scribbler. The writing is printed in real small letters so sometimes I got to guess at what he is saying.

> Sept. 4: Woke up about 6:00 in the morning ready to face another day, a day when I got to do something different. Today I go visit my lawyer in Edmonton.

He spends another couple of pages telling how he had to wait four hours in the lawyer office and then found out they didn't want to see him anyway. He tell too of how he come home real mad and get drunk.

> They going to send me to a doctor who'll try to get me to remember the events of the night I killed my friend Joey Owl. I told them I drank so much I don't remember anything except one scene that's stuck in my mind like it was flashed-up by lightning on the clouds. I can see Joey sitting on the bed in his room asking me to kill him. And I guess I did.
>
> Joey was my friend. We used to get drunk together. I wished I hadn't killed him. But we was drunk and he asked me to. I don't know why he did or I did.

I wonder why Ellsworth want me to read this writing of his. And that's about the first thing I ask him the next time he come by which is about two weeks later. By then his paper is kind of frayed from being carried in the back pocket of my jeans.

"I figure you write down stories, you must be able to read good," is all he say at first. Then after a long silence, "I got nobody to read what I write. I *have* to write these words down. I thought you might understand."

He is still standing in the yard leaning on the door frame even though I invite him in.

"I understand," I tell him. I hope he don't want me to get his words printed up for him. Couple of lady friends of my ma's brought me stories they'd written, and there are rumours that Chief Tom Crow-eye be writing his life story.

Ellsworth don't say no more. He just give to me a few more pieces of paper and walk away.

> Today I feel tight as a string of barbed wire stretched until it ready to break. I miss my kids and my wife. The cabin is cold and I too lazy to light a fire. My wife Caroline went back to her home on the Red Pheasant Reserve. I can't go visit her or the kids. A condition of my bail is that I don't go no more than 50 miles from this reserve. So I'm already part way in prison.

He come back the next day with more yellow paper in his hand. We talk a little at the door. I sure surprised at how gentle he speak most of the time. The guys he used to run with was tough and mean and I figured him for the same. What he write seem more gentle than him in person.

> Troubles are piled on me until I feel like that man I seen in a picture who hold the world up on his hands. Only I'm going down under the weight. Sometimes it would be nice to cry or cuss or scream, just anything to let loose all the heat inside me. I'm

gonna have to blow off steam soon and I'm afraid for what I might do.

Next time he come I was away somewhere and he stuck one sheet of paper in the door-jamb.

Silas, you want to hear a funny joke? My cousin Luke Traveller he say to me one day, "I want to sell my car but it's shot to hell and got a hundred thousand miles on it."

"Take it down to the garage," I say to him. "Get Fred Crier to turn back the speedometer."

Couple of weeks later I see Luke again.

"Hey," I say to him, "you been able to sell your car yet?"

"Why'd I want to sell it?" says Luke. "It only got ten thousand miles on it."

I tell Mr. Nichols, my counsellor up at the Tech School at Wetaskiwin, about Ellsworth, and it is him who give me the magazine I get the idea from.

About the fifth time Ellsworth visit he finally come inside.

"I don't know what else to do so I write some of my trouble on paper. But even then I got to find someone to read it. Look, I killed my best friend. My wife and kids are gone. I'm gonna spend a long time in a white man prison. My lawyer say if I'm lucky I get maybe ten years for manslaughter.

"Only release I know of is to get drunk, or get high on wildwood flower. What I like to do is throw a tantrum, roll on the floor like a little kid; cry and maybe hold my breath. Don't you ever feel like that, Silas? No, I guess you don't. You got everything going for you."

"Sometimes I do," I say. "My troubles ain't serious like yours, but I have to deal with Government, and with people who print books, and I have to write exams at the Tech School. And everybody figure that because I wrote a book I'm rich—I'd make lots more money on the Welfare. And lots of times I feel all empty inside and think for sure I'm never going to be able to write another word. When I get real tense I feel like there be birds fluttering inside me." Ellsworth smile some and lean across the table toward me.

"Silas, I feel so tight all the time. Like I'm hollow and got a pole run between my ears with guitar strings tied to it and another pole across my stomach where the other ends is tied. Some of them strings is gonna break soon, and I'm afraid of the sound of them snapping and of the way they gonna tear up my insides when they do.

"You know what's the most awful, Silas? I can't afford to strike up a close relationship with nobody as long as this trouble hang over me. It would be so nice to. My social worker is Indian and I could like her easy and I think she likes me too. It would be good to have a woman to confide my thoughts to. But it wouldn't be fair. Even if I could see my wife. But her brother talked her into moving. He's a chief at Red Pheasant Reserve in Saskatchewan."

Next day there is more paper stuck in the door when I get back from Tech School.

Hey, Silas, you want to hear about my uncle Clayton Shot-both-sides. He decided he was going to raise sheep but the coyotes kept carrying them all off, so Uncle Clayton got a Government loan through the Indian Affairs and he built the best sheep pens in Alberta. He put up fine-mesh fence too high for coyotes to jump over and too close to the ground to dig under, and strong posts each one braced with a two-by-four. First morning Uncle Clayton get up all his sheep be dead and he got a half-dozen coyotes locked in his pen. What he done was braced the posts from the outside and the coyotes just walked up the braces and into the pen. That was 20 years

ago and Uncle Clayton still get kidded about how he
started Alberta's first coyote farm.

I hardly get that read before Ellsworth come banging
at my door.

"I'm afraid for what I'm gonna do tomorrow night,"
he say to me. "I hear my brother-in-law, should be
bother-in-law, is coming down from Saskatchewan. His
name is Clarence Ahenakew. He bringing his truck and
gonna pick up the rest of my furniture from my house
and haul it away. If it hadn't been for him Caroline
would of stuck with me. Now, even if I get off, I got no
wife or kids or furniture and all because of this fat
brother-in-law who think he's so good because he hold a
job and go to church."

"What did your brother-in-law have against you? He
must of not liked you even before you got in trouble."

"He was sore that Caroline didn't marry a friend of
his, and sore 'cause she moved down to this reserve. I'm
already charged for killing one guy, couldn't make it
much worse if I was charged for killing two."

I figure I got to do what I can for Ellsworth. I've had
this idea for quite a while now ever since I read the
psychology magazine Mr. Nichols give to me, and I hear
Ellsworth talk about how he is full of tight strings. I
know his feeling. Sometimes when I have to put up with
the Government or the Church I feel so helpless, I get so
mad my hands shake.

I even tell my idea to our medicine lady, Mad Etta.

"All white men ain't dumb," says Etta, "just most of
them. That psychology doctor could probably be a medicine man if he was to get some training." And she laugh
and laugh, shaking on her tree-trunk chair. "Problem
with you guys and most Indians now days is that you
don't work enough. If you and Ellsworth had to ride
bareback on a pony for three days to find a buffalo herd,
then kill a couple, cut them up and drag them back to

camp, you'd both be too tired to be nervous. You'd get to sleep for a day then go hunt more food." Etta take a long pull on her bottle of Lethbridge Pale Ale.

"You guys got too much time for thinking. Good hard work would put us medicine men out of business…all old time medicine men had to worry about was drumming up good weather and lots of buffalo. Now people come to me with bad nerves 'cause they feel guilty about hitting their girlfriend or kicking their cat," and she shake sideways on her chair so hard I'm afraid she's gonna spill off.

That night I invite Ellsworth to have supper with us. He make a big fuss over my little sister Delores, say how she remind him of his own little girl.

Right after supper we borrow Louis Coyote's pickup truck and drive to Wetaskiwin to Poffenroth's Auction Store. They have there a sale every Thursday evening. We snoop around look at boxes of clothes, pots and pans, appliances, books, and just plain junk. I pick out what it is we are going to bid on and tell Ellsworth he got to pay half of the money. It is about an hour into the sale before our box come up. I bid it at a dollar and somebody ups it to two—we take it by quarters up to four dollars before the other fellow quit. Ellsworth grumble some as he give me his two dollar share, saying we could of bought a case of beer instead.

It is a big box, used to hold McGavin-Toastmaster Bread, and it take both of us to carry it to the pickup truck and we kind of stagger across the rutted parking lot.

"I think this is about the dumbest idea I ever heard of," says Ellsworth as we drive back toward the reserve.

Once we get there we got a problem. We need use of a cement floor.

First we go to Ben Stonebreaker's place. One of the garages behind his general store, what he use for store canned goods in, have a cement floor. We back the truck up to the garage, pull open the green-painted wood doors, and Ellsworth and me unload the box, what be crammed full of dishes, onto the cement.

Always seem to me that the floor be cement, and guess it was, forty years or so ago when it was built. About all that's left now is little patches of cement like lily pads in a pond of gravel. I take a cup out of the box and toss it down on the floor, but it miss the concrete and skid off to a corner like it been kicked.

"Where else can we go?" I say to Ellsworth.

"Should have stayed in Wetaskiwin they got lots of sidewalks there."

"Ain't something you can do on a sidewalk. People would look strange at white men doing what we going to do—but for Indians they'd have police called in nothing flat."

"I don't see how this gonna do either of us any good, but what about Blue Quills Hall?" says Ellsworth. "Nothing going on there tonight and there's an empty storeroom in the basement."

"I should of thought of that before," I say. I sometimes clean up the hall after it been used and I got a key to the side door.

We load the box back up on the truck and drive down to Blue Quills. The sky is clear; the October moon bright as chrome. We open the side door and carry in the box.

"Be careful we don't break none of these," says Ellsworth, laughing and puffing as he back down the stairs. Most of the basement is used for a kindergarten class. The room smell of chalk and wet mittens. Over in the corner is a storeroom about 8 x 10. We skid the box across the concrete, open the door and pull the string to turn the light on. There are some empty shelves along one side and a beat-up lampshade lay in the corner. The room smell of cement dust and lumber.

"What do we do now?" says Ellsworth.

It seems to me to be awful quiet. I sure wish I had Mad

Etta here to help me start. I close the door. The box is full of all kinds of old dishes: cups, saucers, bowls and a big stack of chipped white and green restaurant plates.

I pick one of them up. "I show you," I say, even though I never done it before either. "You think of somebody you don't like as you bust the dish."

"That's all?"

"You got to try it to see how it works." I hold the heavy green and white plate with both hands and raise it above my head. "This is for the RCMP," I say, and smash the plate down on the floor. It break in about 50 pieces. WHAM is the noise it make and the sound bounce around that room like a hard rubber ball.

"Try it," I say. "Your brother-in-law's the guy who bugs you most. Break one on him." Ellsworth pick up a saucer, lift it up with one hand, "This is for Clarence," he says, quiet like, and toss down the saucer. It break in half and don't make much noise at all.

"Do another one," I say, "only show that you really mad." Ellsworth take another plate and raise it up.

"This is for that Legal Aid lawyer who talk in words I don't understand and make me wait all day in his office," and he break it down hard.

"That's better," I say, and when I look at Ellsworth he has the start of a smile on his face.

"This here's for Chief Tom," I say, smashing a cup so the pieces skip into the corner.

"Can you do somebody more than once?" say Ellsworth.

"Ain't no rules. Do somebody as many times as it take to be not so mad anymore. Loosen up them strings inside you."

Pretty soon we are both making quick trips to the box for plates and cups and bowls. Our voices collide with each other and sometimes we smash things at the same time. It is almost as if we are doing a dance.

I don't know about Ellsworth but for me it is like I

stand naked in the sun. It is like I tear open my chest and
a flock of black birds is flying out one after another,
wings flapping with sounds like someone playing cards
down hard on a table.

We look at each other and grin, yell some, and smash
some more. I grin big as I think that outside the hall all
that smashing must sound like muffled gun shots.

THE MOCCASIN TELEGRAPH

THERE WAS HEAVY snow on the ground the night Burt Lameman did himself a murder up to Wetaskiwin. He'd been around the reserve in the afternoon and stole Robert Coyote's 22 rifle. They say he looked drunk and stoned when he walked into the 7-11 Store on 49th Ave. and shot the clerk. Clerk's name was Bobby something, a white kid with short hair who went to the high school and was saving his money to buy a fancy pair of skis. At least that's what the newspaper said.

Burt didn't say "This is a holdup," or anything like that. He just walked in and shot the clerk, reached over the counter and took $27 from the till, then staggered out into the dark. There were four or five people who seen him do it. He didn't make much of an attempt to get away, just walked a block or two to a small park, with some people following along, keeping him in sight. He kicked in the door to a skating-rink-shack and went inside. A few minutes later the RCMP come along and Burt take a couple of shots at them as they run up toward the shack. RCMP's don't take kindly to being shot at so they blast through the open door with shotguns, rifles and handguns. Burt he end up with enough bullets in him to kill maybe five or six Indians.

So far that seem like just a story of how a bad dude get blown away by the police, but it don't take long for it to turn into something else altogether.

Even around the reserve nobody like Burt very much. He was a bully, a thief, and a liar. That last day he'd drunk some home-brew and sniffed up some angel dust. "He'd swallow a doorknob if somebody told him it tasted good," is what my friend Frank Fence-post say about him.

When they have the funeral for the store clerk, none of us Indians go. White people are feeling ugly, and they look meaner than usual at us when we walking down the streets in Wetaskiwin.

Burt's funeral get held up 'cause there be no money to pay for it. His mother, Mrs. Bertha Lameman, don't have any, and his father been dead for a lot of years. Ordinarily, we'd take up a collection of some kind, but none of us have much sympathy for what Burt done.

Then the AIM people arrive in town. First I seen a couple of cars and a van with South Dakota license plates, and then I seen Gunner LaFramboise, the Alberta organizer for AIM, sitting with four or five cool looking dudes in the Travelodge cocktail lounge. These guys got shiny braids, hundred dollar black stetsons, and wear plastic Indian jewellery. AIM usually stand for American Indian Movement but most people around here call them Assholes In Moccasins. American Indian Movement act kind of like a religion who say everybody who don't believe in them is gonna go to hell. Gunner, when he see me, motion me over to his table. He introduce me to guys from Montana, Wyoming and someplace else, and say they are Crow, Cheyenne, and Blood.

"Week from today we gonna have a funeral for our murdered brother," say Gunner. "You fellows be sure and come and bring all your friends."

"I think you got it wrong," says Bedelia Coyote. "It was Burt who done a murder."

"Maybe," says Gunner with a sly smile. "It never been proved in court. But the RCMP shot him down in cold blood just because he was an Indian. Maybe Silas here," he say, pointing at me, "could write up a story for the newspaper."

"I don't write for newspapers," I say. "And if I did I'd write the truth."

"Wouldn't want you to write anything but the truth," say Gunner. "Sure somebody shot that guy in the store, but a poor Indian just happened to be walking by and he panicked and run when he seen all them people coming after him and then the RCMP executed him," and Gunner give us all a big, innocent smile.

In a day or two the streets of Wetaskiwin begin filling up with more Indians than I ever seen, even on treaty days. And most of them is strangers. There's about 4,000 Indians in the four bands that make up the Ermineskin Reserve, so there's lots of people from Hobbema that I don't know, but I can tell just by looking that most of the Indians walking the sidewalks and darkening the doorways of businesses is strangers. The weather has warmed up, which ain't usual for this part of Alberta in the winter. The air get soft and the streets and sidewalks covered in a black slush. And everywhere is strange and calm just like when the wind dies for a few seconds before a thunderstorm hits.

When I go into the Gold Nugget Cafe, where I work some Saturdays, Miss Goldie, the owner, put me right to work, say she is busier than a weekend even though it only Tuesday.

"People are so quiet," she say. "I know how to handle drunks and troublemakers, but all this silence frightens me."

If it scares Goldie, it scare the TV and radio guys too.

The murder get good play in the *Wetaskiwin Times* and on CFCW, the Camrose radio station, but hardly get a paragraph in the *Edmonton Journal*.

TV, radio, and newspapers always listen to people
who yell loudest, so Gunner LaFramboise and his friends
get a lot of time and space. Gunner take credit for all the
people coming to town, but those arriving sure don't look
like militants. They is just ordinary folks and lot of them
bring along their kids and their campers.

The next night about 11 o'clock, everybody is in bed
when I hear a car stop outside the cabin and lights blaze
bright as the sun shine through the windows. When I
open the door, with Ma, Sadie, and my brothers and
sisters peeking out behind me, it is like the Northern
Lights been squeezed together and pointed at the cabin.

"Are you Silas Ermineskin, the assistant medicine
man?" a white voice say.

I tell them that I am.

"What's going on up in Wetaskiwin? Where are all the
people coming from?" the voice say.

I shield my eyes from the light and by squinting real
hard can see a guy with a camera on his shoulder, and
two or three more people behind him aiming the lights at
me. They've opened up the doors of a white van that say
Canadian Broadcasting Corporation on the side.

"What is it you want to know?" I say. I'm sleepy and
ain't thinking so good.

The voice says something about them coming here
because I had some books printed up, and that somebody
told them I'd make a good spokesman for my people.
Then it repeats the question again.

"Bunch of folks come to a funeral," I say. I've learned
by listening to Chief Tom how to not really answer a
question.

"But there are more people arriving every hour. There
are Indians from as far away as Sioux Lookout in
Northern Ontario, some have come from the Northwest
Territories, Arizona, New Mexico, and Colorado, and
from all over the Prairie Provinces too."

"No law against folks coming to a funeral," I say. I
wish Mad Etta was here.

About this time my friend Frank Fence-post push through the crowd and stand beside me. Frank he ain't afraid of nobody and likes to talk about things he don't know nothing about. He would make a good reporter but a better politician.

"I'm his manager," Frank says, pointing at me. And pretty soon I hear him saying to the TV people, while he smile as if a pretty girl just asked him to her hotel room, "On a bad weekend the bear will eat its own young." I don't know what that means and I know Frank don't, but the TV film it, the Radio people who followed the TV out here, record it, and a couple of newspaper ladies who followed the radio car, write it down like it coming out of a minister.

Frank, he sure is happy to get to talk. "Just call me Chief Frank," he says. He tell one story about how us Indians get our names by being called after the first thing our fathers seen after we was born. It is a pretty good story but end with some four-letter words that catch a radio lady by surprise. I can hear a man's voice, must be all the way back at her radio station, yelling at her.

"Chief Frank, how do all these people know to come here?" ask one TV man who got slick yellow hair, and headphones big as frying pans cover his ears.

"You never heard of the moccasin telegraph?" say Frank, get a surprised look on his face.

"No," say the TV man.

"Well," says Frank, and take a deep breath, and I bet if I listen close I could hear the wheels turning inside Frank's head. "The moccasin telegraph is how white men say us Indians get messages to Indians a long ways away. I let you in on the secret. You know how prairie chickens drum in the underbrush in the fall, and how that sound travel for miles? Well, a wise old medicine man name of Buffalo-who-walks-like-a-man, long time ago mix up some herbs and roots in a porcupine bladder, and use it to tan prairie chicken hides. When them hides is stretched over a special drum why the sound travel for maybe a hundred miles. And it don't make a bump-bump-bump sound like a regular drum, but a quiet hum like the telegraph wires do way out in the country on a quiet night."

All these press peoples look at Frank like they was three years old and he was this Big Bird off the television.

"Messages just hum across the country—go from medicine man to medicine man; tells all the Indians when they are to gather for a pow-wow, or celebration, or in this case Burt Lameman's funeral," and Frank he fold his arms across his chest, look real solemn.

"How many people do you think have arrived so far and how many do you expect by the day of the funeral?" ask a girl with silver hair, so stiff it look like it got glue mixed with it.

Frank screw up his face. "Hey, us Indians is just like the Government. We got different departments. Numbers ain't my department. You ask my friend Silas here about that. Hell, I know so little about numbers I keep my fly open in case I have to count to eleven," and he grin at that radio lady, make sure her eyes get down to see the bulge in his jeans.

The next day Frank's picture on the front page of the *Edmonton Journal* along with the story about thousands of people converging on Wetaskiwin for a murderer's funeral, and they say he was on the CBC Evening News too.

"That was a pretty good story," I say to Frank later. "You're getting almost as good as me at making them up."

"What do you mean making up?" says Frank. "That was all true. Would I lie to the CBC?"

Actually, Buffalo-who-walks-like-a-man was the father of our medicine lady, Mad Etta. And next day Frank he send a television crew up to interview her. My girl, Sadie One-wound was there and say that Etta, who weigh close to 400 lbs., look at the TV crew mean as a bear been got out of her den in February and toss one of the cameramen about 50 feet into the willows. Then she rock that white van back and forth, and if Sadie hadn't talked soft to her and got one of the TV crew to promise her two dozen of Lethbridge Pale Ale, she would of tipped that van right over on its side.

Gunner LaFramboise from AIM follow the radio and TV people around like he was puppy and they got pork chops tied to their ankles.

"You can call it anything you want, but I call it an execution. If it had been a white man in that shack they would have just surrounded it and would have brought in ten social workers, a couple of priests, his parents, aunts and uncles, and his favorite hockey player to talk him into giving himself up."

"Why are you here?"

"Me and my red brothers are here to try and see that justice is done," and he smile real friendly for the camera.

By next afternoon the press people are so desperate for news they now go around interviewing each other.

Frank get to tell his stories over and over and people keep asking me questions. Chief Tom put in an appearance 'cause he can smell a reporter from five miles away, but they get tired of him quick 'cause he don't even know who Burt Lameman was, and all he want to talk about is the Alberta Government oil pricing policies. He don't know nothing about that either but he read off a letter sent to him personal by Peter Lougheed.

Frank he get tired of telling stories and interrupt a guy who got a silver microphone pushed right up into his face. "Hey," says Frank, "I want to show you guys my guitar," and shove under the reporter's nose a little transistor radio which ain't much bigger than a deck of cards, and what he carry in the pocket of his jean jacket most of the time.

"This is a radio," say the reporter, who wearing a top

coat over a yellow blazer, toe rubbers and a red wool scarf about ten feet long. "And turn it off or we'll get feedback," he say in a cross voice.

"You guys too proud to look at a poor Indian's guitar?" say Frank. "I mean it ain't as fancy as what Johnny Cash or Roy Clark play on, but it's the best I can afford."

That announcer quick look over at his assistant who carrying something like a parachute full of batteries on his back. There be black wires connecting the two of them together like they be divers or maybe that special kind of twins.

"It's a radio," the assistant man says.

"Pretend it's a guitar," I say, doing as good as I can to keep a straight face. "He's likely to get mean if you don't."

"That's a really nice guitar, man," says the announcer.

"That's better," says Frank.

David One-wound, my girlfriend's brother, make his living by several kinds of creative borrowing. He carry on his back, all year round, a red nylon back-pack, which hold a car jack, a lug-wrench, and six different kinds of screwdriver. David claim he can take all four wheels off a car or truck in less than four minutes.

While these interviews been going on David One-wound and his friends took off the two far-side tires of the white CBC van, did it so careful even the engineer man inside didn't notice. They carried off the wheels and left blocks of wood under the axles.

Them guys get really mad when they try to drive away and the blocks tip over. They want somebody to call the RCMP.

"What good would that do?" we say. RCMP don't carry no spare wheels. But I bet somebody from around here have spare parts. Chief Frank, why don't you whistle up the One-wound Car Part Company."

Frank he make a face like he whistling but no sound come out. The reporters is real surprised when David

One-wound, and Eddie Powder come from behind the hall, each carrying a tire and wheel.

"Those are our tires," say the reporters.

"Oh, no, those are spare parts we keep around in case of emergency," says Frank, and everyone laugh. "We sell them to you for only a hundred dollars each."

"But they're our wheels."

"You guys don't catch on very quick," says Frank. "Look, to be fair we even take a vote on it. How many say those are Indian wheels, and how many say they are white man wheels?"

Everybody vote for them being Indian wheels, even some of the other reporters.

The funeral: First it was gonna be from the little church on the reserve with Father Alphonse doing the service. Ordinarily, there wouldn't have been 20 people there. Just a few relatives and one or two friends—if Burt had that many. Even militant people like Bedelia Coyote was mad at Burt for giving all us Indians a bad name.

"Who do you figure gonna get remembered and used as an example every time Indians get mentioned?" say Bedelia. "It ain't guys like Mark Antelope, who run in the Commonwealth Games, or Sandra Bitternose, who getting to be a lawyer, or any of the people who got good jobs and stay out of trouble. Burt Lameman's name get thrown up for the next ten years," and Bedelia bang her fist on the table in the Gold Nugget Cafe, make the coffee cups jump.

Next, they move the funeral to the big Sacred Heart Catholic Church in Wetaskiwin, then it get moved over to the Canadian Legion Hall which hold more than 500 people, but as the town get fuller and fuller until it bulge like a gunny-sack filled with hay, the funeral get sent over to the hockey arena. At the arena they put boards down to cover the ice and the church have to hire a carpenter to build an altar. I hear that he build it too wide and tall and they have a hard time gather up enough of their religious rugs and scarves to cover it up.

The night before, all the cafes, stores, and bars was full with Indians; they say motels from Lacombe to Edmonton is full up. But it like the streets full of shadow people who walk quiet as if the slushy sidewalks was made of moss. Nobody get in trouble and the only noise is Gunner LaFramboise and his friends from AIM who set up a card table on the corner of 51st Ave. across from the Alice Hotel and try to sell memberships in AIM. But I don't see nobody buying.

The funeral set for ten o'clock but the arena start to fill up about eight. It got real cold overnight, and the mud of the parking lot, froze solid, look like fancy chocolate, and there be little puddles of water turned to ice and they crack loud as breaking glass when cars and campers crunch across the lot. The cars covered deep with frost and I can see the marks where windows been scraped off.

The TV and radio men have faces red with cold and they slap their arms against their sides while they take pictures of everybody filing in for the service. It funny to see people walking slow into an arena, looking like they just come off a hard day's work, instead of having expectant faces like hockey crowds usually do.

There don't be no hearse. Instead, Gunner hired old Pete Crookedneck, one of the only Indians who still know how, to build a travois. An old white horse, got a big black bow tied to his bridle, drag the travois carrying the coffin, from the funeral home to the hockey rink. Then eight guys, who I guess is all from AIM, 'cause they headed by Gunner LaFramboise, lift the coffin up shoulder high and carry it slow into the arena.

Toward the end of the service, somebody give a signal, I don't see who, but a couple of hundred men stand up in all different parts of the arena and file outside real quiet.

Father Alphonse from Hobbema, do the Catholic burial service, but nothing more, with the priest from

Sacred Heart in Wetaskiwin helping out. I heard that Father Alphonse tell Gunner LaFramboise he have him carted away by the RCMP if he try to speak at the funeral. There be a half-dozen or so RCMP's back behind the altar but they stay mainly out of sight.

All Father Alphonse say about Burt is that it a shame he died so young, and about that time his microphone stop working so if he planned more he couldn't say it anyway.

There had to be close to 6,000 people at that funeral. Seeing that many quiet people send a shiver down my back. But what get to me even more is when we walk outside—right from the front of the arena, clear down to 51st Ave. there be, about every six feet, on both sides of the road, an Indian, stand with his feet at attention and his arms folded across his chest. The old white horse drag the travois and coffin past that honour guard and on to the funeral home where they say Burt going to be cremated.

Bertha Lameman, Burt's mother, and four of her other kids walk along behind the coffin. I hear that AIM bought her a new coat for the funeral.

After the funeral I hear just the end of a interview a radio man doing with Burt's mother.

"Tell me about your other children, Mrs. Lameman?" say the interviewer. She talk a long time but what it amounts to is three of her kids turn out good and three don't. That don't impress the reporter but it impress me; it's a lot better than the average around here.

Later on the bars and cafes fill up again, but people stay quiet. Somebody tell me that for all their trouble AIM only signed up three new members. Pretty soon the cars, pickups and vans head out to Highway 2A and turn either north or south. Some of those people look kind of puzzled on the outside, like I feel on the inside.

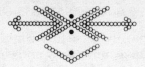

GREEN CANDLES

Big dave baptiste and Victor Powder was trapping partners for a lot of years. They'd go out in the fall, backs loaded down with supplies and if the trapping was good they'd come back in at Christmas, this time with their backs bent down with furs. They each had a long term trapline lease with the Government on land way back behind the reserve fifty miles or so in the Rocky Mountain House country. They kept up a couple of line cabins out there and made themselves a good living. It is nice to see guys who are such good friends that the only thing could break them up would be a woman. And it was.

They weren't the kind of guys you would ever figure to be partners. Victor Powder was a good 15 years younger than Dave Baptiste. Victor be 27 or so and a guy who knew his way around. He is good looking in a kind of mean way and the girls go after him. People laugh and joke that lots of women turn down the covers on their beds when Victor Powder come to town. Vic is slim and like to comb his hair up in a big wave with lots of hair oil. His eyes be kind of wet looking and in the light glisten just like his hair.

Dave Baptiste be about six and a half foot tall. He is a

quiet man and hardly have any conversation to make with anybody. Dave move slow and easy the way a big horse walk in a pasture. His smile be a long time coming but then it is like somebody shine a flashlight on his face, and he never get mean even when he drunk. Dave when he was young was a trapper and a hunting guide. He was the very best there was, so people say, he moved through the bush so good he was like an animal himself. Then for some reason he went off and joined the Army. He was away for a lot of years. It was in the Army that he get to be friends with Victor Powder. A lot of times Dave wear a red bandana tied around his head, made him look like a pirate, and a thick vest made of red fox pelts.

When Victor was about 16 he got caught by the RCMP for doing some breaking and enterings. To keep him from being sent to jail, his legal aid lawyer tell him to tell the judge that he going to join the Army and never be seen around Wetaskiwin no more. The judge take to that idea, figure it be cheaper to let the Indian join the Army than send him to jail.

Big Dave was the only other Indian in the Army unit where Victor got sent. He kind of take Victor under his wing, and when after a couple of years they both get out of the Army, they become trapping partners.

Last winter, they come in around first week of December loaded down with furs. After they sell off, both come away with a pretty big bankroll. They figure to hang around and party for six weeks or so before heading back to the trapline.

In town they hardly ever do the same things. Victor go drinking every night, Dave like to go to the show at the Wheatlands Theatre, then maybe just stop in for a beer or two. Dave be shy around women and never have much to do with them. Victor Powder he got strings on a whole lot of different ladies.

It wasn't a bad thing that Big Dave done. I mean

everybody hear Vic say lots of times how he don't give a care for the girls he go out with.

"Three drinks and drop the laundry. Then move on to the next one," is how he describe his doings with women.

That night there was 7-8 tables of us Indians at the Alice Hotel in Wetaskiwin. Vic, he brought along Juanita Claw as his date but all evening he off dancing with one of the Stonechild girls who ain't even old enough to be in the bar. Last summer Vic lived in with Juanita for a while and they seem to be pretty serious.

Juanita Claw is not real old, 25 maybe. She got married young and had a couple of kids quick, then her husband got himself killed up at a lumber camp near Whitecourt. Tree fell on him is what they say. They buried him right up there in the bush. All Juanita ever got was his duffle bag and a cheque for the hours he worked before he got killed. Guess the Government don't have no money to send home dead Indians. The outfit he worked for wasn't a regular contractor so there was none of this here Workman's Compensation or a pension or nothing for Juanita.

Dave Baptiste had come over to the bar after the show was out and him and Juanita got to talking. Guess that she didn't mind having some attention paid to her, though I think at first it is mainly her who pay the attention. Juanita have quite a few drinks, so she is not so shy as she usually is, and before long they is holding hands across the table top. Then pretty soon they gone and got a taxi to take them the eleven miles back to the reserve and Juanita's cabin.

When Vic ask where they gone we tell him the truth cause we sure don't figure it gonna make any difference to him. He been doing everything but stick it to this young girl on the dance floor, and by the way they acting there sure ain't no doubt about what they going to do to each other as soon as they get the chance.

"I wonder what the hell she sees in him?" Vic say as

his voice get mean and his face get ugly at the news. I would of thought he'd have been happy that Dave find himself a woman.

Victor make the same kind of comment the next afternoon at the pool hall at Hobbema. He tease Big Dave about him getting it on with Juanita the night before, but everybody can tell that it be a cruel kind of tease and not the fun kind. He say a couple of times about how much older Dave is than Juanita.

Big Dave he don't do much but make a shy smile.

But Victor make sure he get to have the final say. He make a little laugh and say how Juanita is not very good in bed, and how if anyone should know he should 'cause of how he's fucked more women in the last week than Dave has in the last ten years. Then he say some real crude things about Juanita, but he say them all like he making jokes, even though every word is pointed like an arrow and aimed at Big Dave.

What happened there was kind of like either "The Fox and the Grapes," or "The Dog in the Manger." I read a whole book of them fables because Mr. Nichols, the guy from the Tech School who read my stories and fix up my spelling and stuff, told me to. Guess I didn't read them good enough 'cause I can never remember which is which.

Dave don't seem to let what Victor say bother him none. The next night he be over at Juanita's at supper time and later on he ask me if I'd borrow Louis Coyote's pick-up truck and drive them up to Wetaskiwin to see the show. On the ride up Juanita rest her face against Dave's chest and she laugh and say that the fox fur tickle her nose. Dave give me $10 for making the drive to Wetaskiwin even though I would of done it for nothing. I offer to come back and get them but he say no, he got lots of money and they'll take a real taxi back to the reserve. That same evening, my girl friend Sadie One-wound babysit Juanita's kids and I spend the evening over there.

Juanita's house ain't really a cabin but one of them places that the Indian Affairs Department have built. It got a kitchen, living room, two bedrooms, a utility room, and have wide siding on the outside that been painted a bright blue. Juanita be a clean housekeeper and she keep her kids neat and see that they go to school every day they supposed to.

Juanita got in her bedroom wallpaper of green leaves and white flowers, both real big, make you feel like you in a jungle or maybe in a Tarzan movie. Me and Sadie make lots of jokes about that and I walk around with a broom in my hand, pretend that it a spear. She also got big green candle be about a foot tall and half as wide, that when it burn smell like incense. That whole room smell a little bit of incense but it get a lot stronger when me and Sadie light the candle. It sure burn pretty but when I go to put it out I get the wax on my fingers and it stain them a bright green.

When Dave and Juanita get back, first thing she do is sniff the air and say, "Hope you didn't get none of that wax on you. It stains." It kind of embarrass me for them to know we been playing around in the bedroom but neither of them seem to mind.

It take that wax about three days to wear off my fingers. Victor Powder, who never miss a thing, make some fun on me at the pool hall, want to know if I been getting it on with Juanita.

I explain what happen.

"I gave her that candle last fall," Vic says. "Cost me six dollars in a store on Boardwalk in Edmonton. I carry it to her place in my bare hands. You ever seen a green Indian?" he say and laugh. Then he talk about how much fun they had fucking in the green light from that candle. He say all this while Big Dave is there.

"How do you like it in the jungle there?" he ask Big Dave, and laugh and laugh when all Dave can do is make a shy smile.

Dave and Juanita have going for them that kind of

feeling where they don't know there is anybody but them around. Dave move himself right in with Juanita and they walk down the road to Hobbema with their arms around each other's waists and kiss sometimes.

"You're not getting serious about her are you?" Victor say to Dave a few days later in the Alice Hotel beer parlour. Dave just shrug his big shoulders and light up a cigarette. Victor smile as nice as he know how.

"Reason I ask is that you and me been partners for a long time now and I don't want to lose you."

"Why do you say that?" says Dave.

"Looks to me like you getting a new partner. Dave, I been there before you. Believe what I say. If you get serious about her, she never gonna let you to trap again." Big Dave don't say nothing but his eyes shift around like they not happy being in his head. Victor real quick to notice that.

"I bet she's talked to you about it already. She lost one man to the bush. She gonna keep her next one close to home."

"We talked some," Big Dave barely whisper.

"Juanita likes her men humble," Victor say. "That's why I got out when I did. Hey, she's a nice lady in her way and I shouldn't of said some of the bad things I said about her, okay? I just do it for your own good. Look all around," Victor go on, waving his hand around the bar, "There's a hundred more Juanitas all over the place. You sample as many as you can when you come in from the bush, and they leave you with lots of nice thoughts for when you out on the cold trapline, but hell, she's *only* a woman. And we're *friends*."

"I thought of fixing up one of the line cabins," Dave whisper again.

Vic clap his hand to his forehead. "She has got to you. She'd never go with you. I bet she never said she'd move with you. She's got kids. Can't take them out where there's no school. She lay that same business on me and

boy I put myself in high gear to get away from her
quick."

Dave shrug and drum his big fingers on the table.

"She'll end up owning you," Vic say. "How you gonna
like being owned? Maybe you could get a job cut brush
for the railway or how'd you like to work in Ben Stonebreaker's grocery store? Or you could go on the welfare,
and Juanita could take you down to the Blue Quills Hall
in the afternoons for tea with the women's club...."

"Nobody owns me," Big Dave say. "Whatever I do, I
do because I want to."

"Sure you do," say Vic, laugh and smile sad, kind of
twist his mouth all out of shape.

The Saturday before Christmas Dave ask me again to
get the truck and with my girlfriend, Sadie One-wound
along, we drive up to the Peoples Credit Jewellers store
in Wetaskiwin, where Dave buy for Juanita a diamond
ring you could choke on if you tried to swallow.

It sure funny how white people treat Indians before
and after they find out they got cash to spend. When the
four of us first go in that store, a man who I guess be the
manager and who wear a grey suit and have a face and
hands the sick colour of newspaper, watch us real close
in case we try to steal something.

We walk along the counters where most everything be
under glass anyway and that man sort of hover just one
counter away and watch us with beady little eyes like a
sparrow.

I wish my friend Frank Fence-post and his girl Connie
Bigcharles was along, 'cause they like to joke around
and make store people think they taking themselves
some five-finger-bargains. One time they got arrested by
the lady store detective in a Woolworth's in Edmonton,
but when the police come and search them they ain't got
no store property on them.

I'd have asked for a lot more, but they settle for a
voucher for $5 each. Frank, he spend all his at the candy

counter. Connie buy a pair of earrings, and then rip-off another pair just to show them she could if she wanted to.

Well, Dave Baptiste take out from the inside pocket of his vest a roll of twenty-dollar bills about three inches thick. Then he tap his big hand on one of the glass cases that be full of diamond rings.

"Hey," he say to the manager fellow, "you got a cash customer here want to look at your rings."

That little man's mouth come into a smile like somebody drawn a happy-face on him and he come over to us just wringing his hands like he was squeezing out washcloths. His eyes eat up the fistful of money that Dave holding as he unlock the case and set out a tray of rings all buried in blue velvet, blink like stars do at night. He tell Dave what a pretty bride he is getting and say quite a few times how she be even prettier with a big diamond on her finger. It is true that Juanita is pretty. Her skin be the light brown colour of tanned leather, her nose wide and soft, and her lips full. She got an awful nice smile and her body fill up her bright green sweater the way a woman should.

Nobody could ever say that Big Dave be pretty. He got a long knobby face like a potato, a high forehead, and a nose that been broke probably more than once.

Sadie, she whisper in my ear, say how come I don't buy her a big diamond ring like that? She say she figures a guy who write stories should make more money than a guy who traps muskrat and fox. But we both know that ain't true, and Sadie push her nose into my neck and we both look wishful at the shiny rings.

It hard for me to figure Victor Powder. He ain't exactly jealous 'cause he at least claim he don't want Juanita no more, and if what he say is true maybe he have a real concern for losing Big Dave Baptiste as his partner and for seeing Dave get himself into a place where he not going to be happy for long.

Still, it seems he go about things in a bad way. "I could have her any time I want her," he say of Juanita one night in the bar. "Once a woman been with me she never turn me away," and he look across at Dave, just dare him to say it ain't so.

I remember once I talk to Mr. Nichols about people who be jealous and he say to me that when someone is jealous of you it don't mean that they love you a lot but that they don't like themselves very much.

That stuff Victor say day after day bother Big Dave even though he try not to show it.

"Just leave us be," he say to Vic one evening.

"I don't want you should mess your life up," Vic answer him and smile real friendly like.

Dave and Juanita make a plan to get married the day before New Year, and they go up to Edmonton to get their blood test and license and stuff.

Victor Powder come stomping into the pool hall, shake new snow off himself. Some of it sit like white feathers in his shiny hair.

"I was just over and seen Juanita," he say for anybody who want to listen. Dave Baptiste look up from the green ball with kind of a scared look on his face.

"We yell at each other all afternoon. She so stubborn sometime I figure I could blow her away," and he throw forward his head, let his oiled hair fall like shoelaces down over his face, then jerk his neck and put it all back in place. "'What the hell do you see in him?' I ask her and she can't come up with nothing but she's 'in love'," and Vic stomp around the hall and talk on and on about all him and Juanita said to one another.

Big Dave finally get up from the bench by the wall looking real unhappy and go out the door while Vic is letting drop something about him coming out of Juanita's bedroom when the kids come home from school. I don't know if Dave hear it or not. The way Vic said it you could take your own meaning anyway.

Night before the wedding us guys decide to have a party for Big Dave. The women that afternoon have shower for Juanita down at Blue Quills Hall.

We have the party at the Canadian Legion. Rider Stonechild, who one time was in the Army, belong to the Legion and we get him to sign us all in as guests of his. Guys who run the Legion wear white shirts and blue jackets and are all about a hundred years old. They wrinkle up their faces to show they ain't crazy about Indians, but they let us in anyway 'cause it been so long since there was a war that most of the Legion men have drank themselves to death by now and their bar never have more than maybe ten people in it. They let us in only 'cause they expect to sell lots of beer, and they is right.

We have us a lot of fun. Everybody is get good and drunk. We make friendly jokes on Big Dave and buy him lots of drinks. Frank Fence-post make him a gift of a French-safe he buy at the joke shop that be big enough to fit over a telephone pole and be white with red maple leafs on it just like the flag. Only person ain't there is Victor Powder.

Along about 11:30 we all get hungry and the guys pool up their money and I get picked on to go get us a barrel of chicken from the Gold Nugget Cafe.

As I come out of the door of the Legion, right there in the driveway under the tall violet streetlight is Victor Powder sit in his brother's car that I guess he borrowed for the night. He is busy doing something and don't see me. I had quite a few drinks or I would of known that something was wrong and maybe I could have stopped it. I should have known by the colour of the light in the car.

When I get back with the chicken, most of the guys are standing around in the parking lot and it easy to see that they is not very happy. Neither Dave nor Victor is within eyesight.

What happen, the guys tell me, is that Victor come in and sit down just after I left. He have a nasty look on his face as he sit across from Dave and put his hands palm up on the table for everyone to see. Then he smile one of them "I told you so" smiles at Dave. Victor's hands was mostly green.

They say Dave run out of the Legion like he got bees in his shirt, and right after, Frank, Robert Coyote, and Rider Stonechild punch Victor's face for him for do such a rotten thing. The Legion people order everyone outside and Victor drive off before he get any more fists laid on him.

A whole lot of people heard the shots and seen Dave walk out of Juanita's house. He still have his 303 held in his big hand as he lope off into the bush. No one ever seen him again. The RCMP even had one of them tracking dogs out to look, but it just runned around in circles. People say Big Dave knew the forest so good he could climb up in the trees and travel without ever touch the ground. I don't think that was true. I figure in maybe ten years or so some kids out hunting will kick across Dave's 303, but by that time the bears will have taken care of everything else.

PARTS OF
THE EAGLE

THE FAMILY NAME was originally Two-brown-bears, and both of Lester Brown's brothers still carry that name. For as long as I can remember Lester and his family just called themselves the Browns. Then, four or five years ago Lester hired himself a lawyer and get his name, and his wife and kids' names, changed from Two-brown-bears to Brown. I remember seeing the change-of-name notice on the back page of the *Wetaskiwin Times* newspaper.

"Why carry around a ten pound name when a two pound one will do?" Lester joke with everybody. But it be kind of a sad joke, and us *real* Indians look down our noses at the Browns, take that name change as just another way Lester Brown have of turning himself into a white man. Lester is a friend of our chief, Tom Crow-eye, who, though he ain't changed his name yet, is whiter than most people been born with pink skin.

Lester is one of the only Indians from here at Hobbema who been all the way through university. He studied first at the Agricultural School at Olds, and later at the university in Edmonton, earn himself a degree in agriculture, which mean he know all about which crops you supposed to plant where, and all about raising cattle, sheep, and pigs.

He put that degree to use too. Lester plow up his half-section of farm land, grow wheat and raise lots of cattle and pigs. He work as hard as a white man, and pretty soon he start sounding like one too. He give little lectures to some of us young guys and even to some adults, about how a man got to work hard to get ahead.

"How long you figure it gonna be before you completely white?" my friend Frank Fence-post ask one day, after Lester stop us on the street to offer advice. Lester Brown don't answer but he sure look hard at us with a mean question in his eyes.

"First you change your name," Frank say, "then you start travelling with Chief Tom, next thing we know you'll be getting white-wall tires for your truck." We already know he *do* have white-wall tires.

Lester kind of growl and stomp off, the steel cleats on his boots making sparks on the sidewalk.

The Browns live in a big white farmhouse, got enough out-buildings could be a little town all by itself. He married himself a girl name of Lena Carry-the-kettle, who been to university and have a degree in home economics, and they got four kids. The oldest, a girl named June, is a close friend of my girlfriend, Sadie One-wound.

Sadie says June is okay and we should lay off her family, but I don't trust a girl who wears dresses, or forty-dollar jeans, and takes dancing lessons.

Lester Brown is above average height, got a barrel chest, wear a straw hat pulled down to ear level, dark green or khaki work clothes. Only thing Indian about him is he wear a big Mexican-silver belt buckle, got three shiny blue stones in it, like islands in a lake. Lately he been letting his hair grow longer than I ever expected he would.

Though they live on the reserve, the Browns don't take part in any of the activities down at Blue Quills Hall.

Lester pay extra money to send all his kids to white man's school in Wetaskiwin, even June who be in high school. "The kids get a better education in Wetaskiwin than at the Reserve School," Lester say. I bet they wish they could all move to an apartment in Wetaskiwin, like Chief Tom done. The Browns ain't thrilled that June's best friend is Indian instead of white.

June wasn't too snooty, I guess. She had a nice laugh, and she talk a lot about how she was gonna study them computers when she get to the university. A couple of weeks ago June drive one of her papa's pick-up trucks into Wetaskiwin for her dancing lesson, on the way back she swerve to miss a dog on the road, drive into the ditch and run the truck up against a culvert. The truck was hardly damaged at all, but June was killed. It sure strange, 'cause I seen pick-up trucks roll about six times, just be scrap when they stop bouncing, and five or six people walk away with nothing more serious than their beer bottles got busted. But slow as the truck was going, June's ribs hit the steering wheel, and one push back into her chest and kill her. Rufus Firstrider was driving a half mile or so behind and seen her swerve and crash, said there wasn't even any blood, not on her blouse or anywhere.

Everybody feel real bad for the Browns on account of the accident. Even people who wish they weren't Indian no more got feelings. They belong to the Catholic Church in Wetaskiwin, and the church is full of more Indians than it seen for a long time, the day of the service. The coffin covered with a yellow rug of some kind, while the Browns sit in the front row dressed like dummies you see in department store windows in Edmonton.

A lot of us go back to Brown's farmhouse after the funeral. Most of the people bring food with them and somebody set up a coffee urn like you see in restaurants or at church picnics. There is about as many white people there as Indians. I come with Sadie, and Frank

Fence-post come with me. Frank ain't a good person to
have at a serious party where there is white people.

Most white people don't see Indians up close too often,
so when they do they ask lots of questions, most of them
silly. A big white lady in a purple dress that about seven
sizes too small ask Rider Stonechild if he can forecast
the weather. She say she hear all Indians can tell how
good or bad a winter we going to have by signs in nature.
When Frank hear that, he push right in in front of Rider
Stonechild, put his hand on the fat lady's big, blotched
arm and say, "I am Duck's Breath; hunter, guide, car
salesman, and weather forecaster. For $20 I will tell you
all my secrets."

"Well, I'm not sure I want to pay," say the white lady,
and she look suspicious at Frank. "Do you forecast
weather by the way animals store food, and grow winter
coats?"

"Wish I could grow a winter coat," says Frank. "Nice
full length leather is what I'd grow. Instead I got to steal
from the Goodwill Store. But I use the rock method to
forecast weather."

By this time he got half a dozen white folks around
him.

"I take a little rock, nice and smooth, weigh maybe a
pound. I tie a string around it, hang it from a fence rail. If
the stone is wet, it's raining. If it's dry, it ain't. If it's
swinging, it mean the wind is blowing. If there's a
shadow under it, that mean the sun is shining. If it's
white on top, that mean it snowed. For only $20 each I
teach you guys how to forecast like that." That ain't very
funny, but what is funny is that white people don't know
whether to believe him or not. If a white person said
what Frank did, everyone would laugh and say, "How
silly." It never occur to them that us Indians have a
sense of humour.

Another time somebody ask Fraser Cuthand how he
come to have a name like that. Before he can answer
Frank butt right in. "I asked my papa that when I was

little," says Frank, "and he say, 'Well, son, us Indians is named after the first thing the mama or papa see after the baby is born. There was a bright moon the night your sister was born so we called her Golden Moon. There were three horses in the corral the day your brother was born so we called him Three-white-horses. Why do you ask, Two-dogs-fucking?'" The white people sure don't know how to handle that. As Frank would say, they stand around don't know whether to pee or go blind.

As each person leave that gathering they shake hands with Mr. and Mrs. Brown, tell them how sorry they are. Sadie, because she was a special friend of June Brown, stay late. About eight o'clock, Mr. Brown look around and see there is mainly relatives left, or close friends like Sadie, or friends of close friends like me.

"It's been a long day," he say with a sigh. "I'm gonna go to bed now." Nobody say anything, but the people who can see him where he standing at the foot of the stairs, nod their heads to show it is a good idea. Lester Brown climb those stairs like he real tired.

I hear Frank giving Chief Tom a bad time about something. The chief is trying to argue by quoting some of the Government information he always spouting out, but I hear him saying that something is *irrevelant,* and too he talking about "the two *spears* of influence."

"Hey, Chief Tom," say Frank. "I hear when it time for you to go to the happy hunting ground that you gonna die in your own arms. Is that true?"

"Hmmmf," say Chief Tom, and he gather up his girl-friend Samantha Yellowknees, and go home.

About an hour later I'm getting tired myself. Sadie and the other women have gone to the big recreation room in the basement. Frank Fence-post is eating what left of the cake and sandwiches. I'm not sure whether it would be polite to turn on the television, even though Mr. Brown got cablevision, and I sure would like to run the dial over them fifteen or so channels.

Instead, I decide to go look around the farm, not that I

could see much in the dark. It is a pretty, pale night, the moon turn everything silver and blue, and the Northern Lights bubble across the hills of stubble to the north. When I look back the house is white as a ghost and glow like foxfire in the bright darkness. I heard that the white aluminum siding for the house cost $12,000 all by itself.

It is real peaceful in the yard, really pleasant after listen to people talk all day. I walk alongside the corral which got only one old pony and a milk-cow in it. They move a little, the cow raise her head a couple of times so I can hear her hide ripple. Past the corral is a little ravine full of scrub poplars and red willow. I figure to walk across it and maybe climb to a hill where I can get a good view of the Northern Lights.

I walk down the side of the ravine, the dry leaves crackling loud. Then off to the right something catch my eye. What is odd is that there ain't nothing there. I mean there is a piece of ground at the foot of the ravine, a flat spot about 6 x 4 that been scraped clear of leaves, and recently too, because it don't look like even one has blown back where the ground been swept.

I stop and stare at that spot for a minute, try to figure what it could mean, when something happen that scare me as bad as I ever been scared. That piece of bare ground creak and begin to rise in the air. I know that some people, like our medicine lady Mad Etta, are able to do magic, but I don't figure Etta to be anywhere around here. I could run, but I don't, my curiosity keep my feet dug in the ground like shovels. That slab of ground rise up until it at a right angle to the earth. I am maybe six feet behind it.

For a minute I can't tell what is happening, then I am able to see that what is rising is sort of a cellar door, and that there is somebody crawling out on the other side. I know there ain't really creatures that live in the earth, but still my heart sound like somebody dribbling a basketball on hardwood. I see the shape of a man pull himself from what must be a hole. He set something on the ground, turn and grab the edge of the door to close it down. But as he does he stare straight ahead and what he see is me staring back.

"Sorry," I stammer. "I was just going for a walk."

"Who is it?" say the voice of Lester Brown.

"It's Silas," I say.

"Oh," he says, and I can hear him relax his body. "I'm glad it ain't one of my family. They got no idea…" Whatever he set on the edge, he quick push into the pit.

"I was just going for a walk," I say again. "Probably best if I keep right on going." Everybody got a right to their secrets, I figure.

"No. It's okay," Lester Brown say, after a few seconds. "You hang around with the Old Woman. This might be good for you to know."

By 'the Old Woman' I know he means Mad Etta. I'm supposed to be Etta's assistant, but she is pretty slow to teach me things. "She figures she going to live forever," is the way Frank Fence-post put it. "Damn right," Etta say to that, and she grin big, her belly shaking when she laugh.

"Come over here," says Lester Brown.

I move toward him, my legs still stiff, my feet dragging through the crusty leaves make me sound like a quiet running motorcycle.

"Hear you clear to Hobbema and beyond," he say. "Nobody ever learn you how to walk quiet?"

"My friend, Old Joe Buffalo, he showed me when I was a kid. But I'm wearing white man's shoes today. And you scared me, rising up out of the earth the way you did."

"Come around here and I show you what I got."

As I move closer, the first thing I smell is leather. Lester Brown is dressed in soft, brown leather, jacket and pants. He wear moccasins, have his hair tied at the back with a thong, and look to me like he wearing the beginnings of a breast-plate, whether it been bought in a store, or is hand made from peeled birch or willow is hard to say.

"My first idea was to send you away, maybe even threaten you to keep you quiet. But I know if I did you'd tell your friends, and word would get back to my wife and kids…" He brace himself on that upright lid and jump back into the pit, not making a sound. The inside lumber is white and it easy to see it solid built.

"I got something down here I bet you never seen before." He stop a second again before he bend to the bottom of the pit. "I'm really glad it's you, Silas, and not your noisy friend, who found me out."

I'm not sure what it is I have found. I'm bent forward from the waist looking down into a dark pit, the size of a grave or bigger. For just a second I have the thought that maybe he just being nice so as to get me close and do me in. My nose catch the odour of herbs, like at Mad Etta's cabin, mixed with the damp and leather smell. All I can see is the top of Lester Brown's head; he don't wear a hat now, and the moon glint off the oil he always wear on his hair.

"See this!" and he lift something from the bottom of the pit, his hands held out in front of him, palm up like he was carrying a tray. The thing he holds is right by my feet. All I can see is a mixture of dark and light.

"Touch it!" say Lester Brown, holding it close by my ankles.

I reach down. What I feel is soft and slick and scary. I pull my hand back quick as if I been shocked by electricity or touched something dirty.

When I lean down and look close, I see what I touched was feathers, my hand feeling with the grain so they felt smooth as enamel.

Lester Brown let out a little laugh, a quiet one like he clearing his throat.

"Indians prayed to the eagle since the beginning of

time," he say. "Eagles are the best hunters, the fastest, the fiercest. You ever seen one dive for a rabbit? It fly like a knife cutting the air. They hit a rabbit so hard it don't even squawk. Once I seen two rabbits side by side, one get carried off by an eagle, but it happen so quick the other just hop a couple of steps and start eating again. An eagle hit hard and fast and fatal."

Strangest thing to me is that in the middle of that speech Lester Brown lapse into Cree. I would of thought he forgot his Cree-speaking. His kids don't speak our language at all, although the last few months June been getting Sadie to teach her a few words.

"I never seen an eagle but from a distance," I say. I seen them circle high up, like big, dark alphabet letters. Sometimes, way out on the prairie, I see their shadows on the hills, dark as cattle brands.

"Shake hands with a real one," says Lester.

I reach down and touch the feathers again, my hand feel like it is stroking silk. My eyes are pretty used to the dark by now, so I see what Lester offering up to me is not a live eagle but the carcass of a dead one.

"You're not supposed to have that, are you?" I hear myself saying. There are laws of all kinds against killing eagles, or selling their feathers; I think it even illegal to have eagle feathers in a headdress, no matter how you claim you have got them.

Lester make that little laugh again. "You never done anything that the white man says is illegal." Then he sort of unroll that eagle for me to see; the head is white, the beak shine yellow, the rest of the body is the colour of dark tree-bark, except for the legs, which again is bright yellow. I bet that bird got over a six-foot wing-span.

Mad Etta know how to preserve a bird the way Lester Brown done this eagle. All the insides and meat and stuff is gone, but the bones and feathers and skin is there, all cured with herbs, tanned and preserved. If we was still to have old-fashioned kinds of ceremonies, why a warrior could wear this eagle skin over his head and look like the fiercest man in the tribe. Used to be an Eagle Society in our Ermineskin Tribe, but most of the societies died out a long time ago, or got to the point where the members meet at Blue Quills Hall, play cards and drink beer.

"I guess I've done a few illegal things," I say, and it is my turn to laugh quiet.

"It is for my religion," Lester say, looking down at the eagle.

"I thought you was Catholic," I say. I'm sorry as soon as I say it. I got to remember to think before I say things that embarrass me. Mad Etta, she tell me, "When someone say something to you, keep your mouth shut until you repeated it once in your head, then if you still don't know what to say, repeat it again out loud. It give you time to think and people like to hear their own words repeated back to them."

"I thought I was too, at one time. Weren't you?" say Lester.

"Government have me listed as one. I think they just list all Indians as Catholic. None of my family ever go to church."

"At one time I figured the more I could imitate the white man the better off I'd be. That's what they taught us at the Reserve School, and at the church. Taught the same thing at the university. They show you how to keep the land under control with chemicals and crop rotation—they don't come right out and say so, but they imply that the old ways ain't no good. You ever hear what Poundmaker say about the white man? 'The land is not his brother but his enemy.' The light has been slow coming to me, Silas. Once a man commits himself to the white man's way he's trapped. He can't undo a whole lifetime of teaching, like maybe taking off a shirt. I married a good woman who likes to do things the white way. I sought out that kind of woman. I can't bring myself to tell any of my family that I've come to believe in the old ways again."

Lester Brown climb up from the pit, still holding the eagle carcass.

"Know the first part of the eagle that I put in my medicine bundle?" he ask.

I shake my head.

"The tongue." And he pat the fat leather pouch what dangle from his belt. "The Old Woman showed me how to preserve it. It look fresh as the day I killed this eagle."

"I never knew that Etta…"

Lester Brown smile. "When I was real troubled about the way my life was going, I went to see the Old Woman. Knocked on her door in the dark of night, after making sure no one was awake to see me; I was that ashamed of what I was doing."

"I never knew," I say again.

"The Old Woman promised me. Her word is solid as the mountains. It was her idea for me to get this eagle. I mean even though I know what the white man knows, I still believe in the power of the eagle. To our people, in the long past, birds were magic because of their flight, their music. I killed this eagle with an arrow," Lester say, holding up the carcass and spreading the wings. "Had to learn to use the bow like a real warrior. After I killed it I did something the Old Woman taught me. You know sometimes she come out to the hills deep in the night. We sit in the wheat field, watch the stars and listen to the life all around us. After I killed this eagle I talked to it. I apologized for killing it; I told it why I had to kill it, and how it was gonna serve a grander purpose than it ordinarily would have. And I asked it to forgive me for shortening its life."

"And did it?"

"I got a feeling like fresh spring water was flowing

where my blood used to be, and I suddenly was able to hear and see and taste everything clearer than I ever could before. I took that as a sign."

"You should tell the rest of your family. They'd understand. They're Indians."

"I wasn't exactly telling the truth when I said nobody in the family knew. There was June…" and he stop, the lines on his face deepening, his grief like war paint, there for me to see. "She found me out the same way you did. After that she would come down here with me late in the night. June is…was smart, she went to Edmonton to the university, found some books on Indian history and customs. Those books had stuff in them that even the Old Woman didn't know. They wrote about *all* the parts of the eagle, and how each part have a significance in Indian religion. She copied down the list and her and me memorized it."

"I'm really sorry about June," I say.

"She had her own medicine bundle. I sneaked it into the coffin when I had the chance. She would of liked to be buried like an Indian instead of a white, but I don't have the nerve yet to do what I have to."

"June was good as you at keeping secrets. Sadie was her close friend and I didn't know…"

"After death, the spirit is carried away by an eagle. Did you know that?"

"I guess," I say.

"It got to be arranged just right. The Old Woman must have had some vision of what was going to happen. Otherwise why would she have told me to get an eagle. Did she ever mention…"

"Etta's secrets are secrets," I say.

"Yeah," says Lester Two-brown-bears, nodding solemnly. "I'm going out to the big hill," and he point off to the north. "To where I can see all the way to the mountains on a clear day. I got to see that her spirit get carried off proper." He stare at me, his face still solemn.

"If you want, you could come along. I'll teach you the Spirit Ceremony, and the parts of the eagle and what they mean."

I look out across the silver fields toward the hill he is talking about. "I'd like that," I say.

THE SENSE SHE WAS
BORN WITH

ABOUT THE UNHAPPIEST thing that could of happened to
Ben Stonebreaker, did. His only daughter, Adele, run off
with a white man. Ben Stonebreaker hates white men.
He hate them even before it was okay for us Indians to
do that. Up to a few years ago Indians was supposed to
do everything we could to be white, like forget about the
old ways and try to learn to farm and hold jobs just like
white men.

Then the Government decide it is okay for us to be
Indians again, and that we should be proud of all our old
ways and customs, and that if we want to be rude to
white men that is okay too, 'cause they been rotten to us
for such a long time that now we should get a turn.

Ben and his wife own the Hobbema General Store.
The store have a sign on the front say Salada Tea on
each end and in the middle in red letters is General Store.
Underneath in smaller letters it say B. Stonebreaker,
Prop. Hobbema is right on the highway but hardly any
white people stop there 'cause they all know it is an
Indian town and they afraid maybe they get scalped or
something. Ben like to make a laugh and say that when
a white man do stop in he leave him wait for ten minutes

59

at the counter even when he not busy which is just about all the time. Ben run one time against Chief Tom Croweye to see who be chief of the tribe. Ben lost 'cause it was still the days when Indians was supposed to want to be white. Chief Tom is so white he don't even remember the days when he used to be an Indian.

Adele was fifteen when she run off and about three years older than me. I remember seeing her sometimes when us kids used to hang around the store. She was wide-hipped, dreamy-eyed, and used to lean on one of the old glass display cases on her elbows, smoke a cigarette, and look across at the side wall of the store like she seen something that nobody else did.

The guy she left with was a magazine salesman. He was maybe twenty-one and come around the reserve saying he was working his way through college, though he sure don't look or talk like he been to college. He have one eye always all squinted up and can smoke a whole cigarette without ever taking it out of his mouth. He also got two tattoos on each forearm and a dagger on the back of his left hand. I remember that his hair was so blond that it looked like soft ice cream piled up on his head, and that he showed some of us guys how to throw a jack-knife by laying it flat on the palm of our hand. While he was here he hung around the store, leaning on the counter drinking Coke and teasing Adele about her freckles.

A year later that magazine company was still sending out magazines and bills to people who never even seen the salesman. What we guess he done was looked at the Voter's List what was nailed to a telephone pole, then made out a whole lot of orders and signed them all himself. Nobody I know ever heard his right name though he called himself Bunty or Bucky, I was never sure which. He was only here two days all told and when he left Adele Stonebreaker went with him. Some say they caught the southbound midnight bus for Calgary, others say they seen them hitchhiking on the highway toward Edmonton. Anyway, nobody ever heard of Adele anymore until a few weeks ago when she come walking into her papa's store right in the middle of the day.

Me and my friend Frank Fence-post was looking at some cowboy boots in the dry goods section of the store.

"Mama?" Adele say. It is Mrs. Ben Stonebreaker who is behind the counter. She is a heavy lady with two grey braids the colour of melting snow.

Mrs. Stonebreaker say something in Cree, come waddle around the counter and hug her daughter. Adele ain't changed so much, her hips is some wider and her breasts bigger but she still have that far off look on her face.

"This here's Caroline," Adele say, nodding to the little girl she hang on to by the hand. Mrs. Stonebreaker kneel down and hug and kiss the little girl some and talk to her in Cree.

"She don't understand Indian, Mom. I never spoke a word of Cree since I left."

It is about then that Ben Stonebreaker come in from the back yard. He stop in the doorway getting his eyes used to the dark of the store.

"Ben, it's Adele. She's come home." It hard to see Ben's face in the doorway. With the bright light behind him he look like about seven foot of black shadow that say, "My daughter's dead."

"No she's not. She's right here."

"I said she was dead," Ben repeat and I guess we all know what he mean by that. After Adele run off he go around mean as a boil for months, take a punch at the face of anybody who even mention the name of Adele to him.

Ben Stonebreaker is tall and walk tall. He have silver-white hair that come to his shoulder and he tie it back with a buckskin head band. He wear a soft leather jacket with fringes hang down all around, black pants, and cowboy boots with flying eagles carved on them. His eyes be deep set and crow-black, his nose straight and fierce.

He start to turn away, then stop, "What's that?" he say, and point to where Caroline is peek from behind the big leg of her mama's jeans.

"That's your granddaughter," Mrs. Stonebreaker say in Cree, in a real harsh voice.

"My daughter's been dead for eight years. I can't have no grandchild. Even if I did she'd be half white."

He ain't wrong about the last part. Caroline be Métis all right. She look about seven, got her mama's heavy legs and high cheekbones, but her skin be a pale brown, like maybe she only a white person with a sun tan. She got light blue eyes and her hair is coarse like Indian, but it is an almost grey colour like it couldn't make up its mind. There can't be no doubt about who her daddy was.

"Get them out of here," Ben say to his wife. "Don't want them on my property."

He get a good argument from his wife about that. I never heard Mrs. Stonebreaker raise her voice before. Guess she is like any lady animal who is quiet and nice until you attack her young.

Ben finally stomp out to the yard where he got a couple of garages and a storage shed, say he suppose they can stay for a day or so as long as he don't have to look at them.

"What about…?" Mrs. Stonebreaker say to Adele, and it ain't hard to figure who she is ask about.

"He got in bad trouble, Mama. Caught him selling drugs of some kind. Got sent off to P.A., say he be old before they let him out." Adele shrug her shoulders. That be the longest speech I ever heard her make before or since.

"Don't Grandpa like me?" I hear Caroline say. Her face cloud up and look sad as a mud puddle. "I know I ain't dead," she insist, "and neither are you," she say to her mother.

"Shhhh," say her mama. Then the three of them go to

the back of the store and upstairs where Mr. and Mrs.
Stonebreaker live, leave me and Frank stand all alone in
the store.

"Silas let's load us up with stuff," say Frank. "We take
it down to the Texaco Service Station and sell to people
who stop for gas," and he's piling his arms full of jeans
and shirts, and he got a pair of cowboy boots in each
hand.

"Ben got enough trouble today without nobody rip off
his store," I say, but while I saying that I gather up some
shirts and about ten pairs of Stanfield's underwear, the
long woolly kind with buttons down the front and a flap
in the rear.

The store be dark and smell of coffee, leather, and the
linseed oil that been poured on the floor boards. As we go
out the front door I flip the lock so that somebody else
don't get a chance to steal anything. We sit on the front
step for a while, Frank and me, and take the price tags
off the clothes, then we walk around to the back of the
store where Ben Stonebreaker is sitting on a box look
like he just lost his only friend.

"Mr. Stonebreaker," I say, "we got here some five-
finger bargains we get from up at Robinson's Stores in
Wetaskiwin. We was wondering if you might like to buy
them from us?"

Frank and me we hardly ever done that kind of thing
but some of the guys do. Ben he buy stuff that been got
by creative borrowing, but only if it been ripped off from
a white-man store.

"What you got?" he say and eye us up and down with
his black eyes.

"Some good shirts and stuff," we say, and lay it out on
a packing box for him to see. He look it over careful.

"Give you a dollar each," he say. "Fourteen pieces plus
$5.00 a pair for the boots."

"We can get more than that sell to tourists down to the
Texaco Service," say Frank.

Ben shrug his shoulder. "Okay, fifty dollars for the

lot," and he reach in his back pocket for his wallet. I ain't let him look at the last pair of boots yet where I left on the bottom his own price tag. He turn over the boot just as he start to count out the money and he catch on awful quick.

"You selling me my own stuff," he yell.

"We just show you what we could of done. Like you always teached us we don't rip off an Indian."

He smile some when he see that we was just joking with him. We walk with him into his storage shed where he got an old pop cooler with some beer bottles sit in rusty water. Ben crack us each a beer.

"I hoped someday I'd have me some grandsons grow up like you guys. Somebody could help with the store," Ben make a big sigh and his shoulders kind of drop forward.

"That little girl's cute," I say.

"She's white," say Ben.

"Still I bet you happy to have your daughter back."

"Adele ain't got the sense she was born with." He take a big pull on his beer. "And what kind of a name is Caroline?"

"What kind of a name is Ben?" say Frank.

"Or Frank or Silas or Adele," I say, "they is all slave names."

Ben shrug his shoulder again. "I tell you what I do," he say, taking another drink from his beer. "I give you guys each two dollars and a pack of cigarettes if you help me straighten up this here shed. I'm getting too old to lift big boxes no more."

While we be helping, Caroline come outside to where we are. She nose around everything just like a cat that been put in a strange place.

"Are you my uncles?" she says to Frank and me. We tell her who we are. Ben pretend she ain't there at all.

"Mama says I'm supposed to stay away from Grandpa, but I want to look at him. I never had a Grandpa before," and she squint up one blue eye and look at Ben Stonebreaker. "Can you shoot a bow and arrow?" She don't wait for an answer. "Mama says you and Grandma are real Indians. Real Indians are supposed to be able to shoot a bow and arrow," and she say that serious like she reading it from a book.

"And take the scalp off little kids," say Frank, take quick the knife from his belt. Caroline run off yelling but it easy to see she only pretend to be scared.

Twice a week the truck from the grocery wholesale in Edmonton bring supplies for the store. Ben pay me a dollar or two to carry them into the shed, and sometimes to stock the shelves in the store.

Caroline is always around. She is like my littlest sister, Delores, seven going on sixty-five. She learn how to make change real quick. She be too short to reach the old cash register with keys like bottle caps, but she got a stool and sit up on it on her knees and count out change faster than anyone but Ben. Pretty soon Adele don't even have to watch her and can lean on the counter the way she used to do, gaze far away and smoke a cigarette. Ben Stonebreaker he stay in the shed or upstairs when Adele and Caroline is in the store. He make sure that wherever they is he isn't.

Adele ain't gonna be long without a man. Rufus Fire-in-the-draw, Moses Blanket, and a couple of other rodeo riders spend a lot of time around the store. It sure good for the Coke and cigarette business, and Adele get about a half a dozen invites to the Saturday dances at Blue Quills Hall.

School start after the Labour Day holiday and things be pretty good except Ben Stonebreaker still don't admit he got a granddaughter.

One day Ben and I unpacking boxes when Caroline come home from school. She be all dressed up like an old time Indian got her hair in braids, fierce paint on her face, a head band, and a pretend-buckskin skirt of brown construction paper. "See, Grandpa," she say, "they made me into a real Indian," and she look up at him squinting one eye and smiling like a puppy want real bad to be petted.

"If I dress up in a white-man suit, tie, and funny shoes, does that make me a white man?" Ben say, not to Caroline but to me.

"Only if you're Chief Tom," I say. Ben and I have a good laugh about that. Chief Tom be what Indians call an apple: red on the outside but white on the inside. Caroline go away with her head down and it sure make me sad to see that.

Another day we're working in one of the garages and Caroline is dig way down behind some boxes in a back corner. "Can I have one of these, Grandpa?" she say. All I can see of her is her legs like two sticks of brown suede pumping the air. Her skirt is up over her back. She got on yellow panties.

"No," say Ben Stonebreaker without even turn to see what it is she want.

Caroline drag up from that corner a cardboard with two dozen yo-yos fitted on it. When Ben see what it is, it start him off.

"Silas, them there is a good reason for hate white men. Four or five falls ago every kid on the reserve want one of them yo-yos and I ain't got none. Next spring this guy come around selling them, say all the kids gonna want them again, so I buy four cardboards of them. One's in the store with one gone off it, the other three is back there. That salesman *knew* but he sell off his junk to a dumb Indian."

"My daddy used to be the yo-yo man," say Caroline.

"That the truth," say Ben Stonebreaker and his face rearrange itself into a sad smile.

"Can I have one, Grandpa?" Ben pretend he don't hear.

I look at the cardboard to see the numbers in the top

corner, 24-50-89. From work around the store I know that mean that there's 24 yo-yos on the cardboard, that Ben paid fifty cents each for them and is supposed to sell them for eighty-nine cents, or more if he can get it.

"Will you sell me one for fifty cents?" I ask. Ben grumble some but say he guess he will. I pick a shiny green one the color of a young apple, take it off the cardboard and give it to Caroline.

She get down off the boxes, wind up the string and make that yo-yo do everything but talk. My friend Frank Fence-post can do things like that too. He can loop-the-loop, walk-the-dog, sleep-the-baby, and all those tricks. When I run one down the string it just lay there like the cord was made of spaghetti. "Thank you, Silas," Caroline say as she buzz that thing past my ear a couple of times. Ben look mean at me but he don't say nothing.

A few days later I walk by the school at noon hour and I see a crowd of kids in a circle. In the middle is Caroline and she buzz that yo-yo I gave her in circles around her head like a big dragonfly and do about every trick I ever seen done and a few more besides. She give the kids a little talk too. She have one eye all squinted up and she tell them how her daddy teached her these tricks and how they can all learn to do the same tricks as her, easy, if they is just get a genuine Land Of The Rising Sun yo-yo just like hers, and she say they is only $1.25 down at her Grandpa's store.

In the store that afternoon, I see the price on the yo-yos been marked from 89¢ to $1.25 and that over half the cardboard is empty already. For all the rest of the week kids is bring in pop bottles and cases of beer bottles and take out a yo-yo in trade. By Friday afternoon we have to dig out from the back of the storage shed the other two batches of yo-yos.

When I come to work I see Caroline is out front of the store do tricks and teach other kids how to use their new toys, and not just kids. My friend Frank Fence-post buy

two, one for him and one for his girlfriend Connie Bigcharles. They zip them around see how close they can
come to each other's noses. I take one turn with Frank's.
The yo-yo run down the string and lay there on the
ground like it made of Jell-o.

Later on Caroline come back where me and Ben is
unpacking boxes.

"Come here," he say to her, and look down on her face
with his black eyes. Caroline squint up one eye and look
back at him. His face look like an old vase that going to
fall apart with age. But it don't fall to pieces when it
smile a little.

"You a pretty smart little girl," he say, and pick her up
by under her arms and raise her face up to his. When she
reach her arms around his neck he don't make no move
to stop her.

"You really love me, Grandpa. I could always tell."

"Somebody in the family got the sense they was born
with," Ben say and hug Caroline again.

I go in the back door of the store to get me a Coke.
Don't suppose Ben would want me seeing him being so
friendly with anyone who was even half white.

THE BALLAD
OF THE PUBLIC
TRUSTEE

LAST WINTER MY friend, Old Joe Buffalo, who had lived for most a hundred years, died. He had no relatives left; he outlived three wives and his only daughter, Ruth, killed herself maybe ten years ago.

I guess you could say I was his closest friend. We done some secret things together over the years, and I even helped him die the way he wanted, like a man and a warrior, not like an old squaw in a white man's hospital.

"Who's gonna pay for this, Welfare, or the Indian Affairs?" ask the man at the funeral home in Wetaskiwin.

"Old Joe be able to pay for his own funeral," I say, and take out a bank book Joe kept in a drawer in his kitchen table, show that he have over $40,000 in the Bank of Montreal in Wetaskiwin.

The funeral man look real pleased. He got sad bags under his eyes like a dog, and skin the colour of newspaper.

"Are you a relative?"

"No. Just a friend."

"Well, send a relative around to sign the papers and pick out the coffin. Tell them to go to a lawyer and apply to get his will probated." He say this to me in a loud voice in case I don't understand.

"He don't have no relatives," I say.

"None?"

"None at all." He don't seem to believe me until I explain that Joe never had no brothers or sisters, and that everyone else close to him is dead.

"That's bad," say the funeral man, bump his pink palm against his white forehead. "That means the Public Trustee will be involved. It may take years before we get paid."

"Hey, don't worry," I tell him. "Old Joe he let it be known he want his land and stuff to go to me. I'll pay you soon as the bank let me at the money."

He smile at me like I was a dog just used his leg for a lamp post. "If you're not a relative and he left no will, you'll never get a cent of his estate." I never thought much about that before. Old Joe tell me what he want done, and his word be worth more than that $40,000 in the bank. But the funeral man's words get to me, and as I leave there, I feel a little like I did the time I got thrown off a bronc at the Rimbey Rodeo: I lay on the ground and I could see everybody standing around me and I could hear them talk, but I couldn't move or speak, and I felt like I was never gonna be able to breathe again.

Joe's 160 acres is all paid for and worth more money than I ever dreamed. Me and my girlfriend, Sadie One-wound, gonna live there in Old Joe's cabin, and I either farm the land or let it stay rented. And I could buy us a car...

But I stop that daydream. I should of knowed the white man going to rip me off if there any way it can be done.

Back at the reserve, I run right to Mad Etta our medicine lady, find her sit on the tree-trunk chair in her cabin, drinking coffee right out of her grey-enamel coffee pot.

I tell Etta what the funeral man told me.

"Who is this Public Trustee guy?" she say.

"I don't know. Some Government man, I guess."

"Well, you find out and take me to him. Old Joe told me how his possessions was to be divided up. That Mr. Public Trustee will want to know."

Old Joe promised me, ever since I was a boy of ten or so that one day when he's gone the farm will be mine. I helped him with his chores and stuff, and he teach me what he know of the old ways of our people. Me and Sadie sometime sat around his cabin when Joe was outside, pretending it was our own place and talk about how we manage it. Sadie want first of all to get bright coloured wallpaper, like she seen at the Robinson's Department Store in Wetaskiwin, and curtains for the window, the kind on a string so's you pull them back and forth.

We have to go all the way to Edmonton to find this Public Trustee, and then we find it ain't one person but a whole department. They located in one of the big Government buildings downtown, and when we get there Etta and me we talk to a pretty girl, have a red ribbon in her hair, who say she get somebody look after us.

The man she send out smell like cherry candy, and he be an Indian, only one of those that come from the Pakistani Tribe on the other side of the earth. I always wonder why the Government offices be full of those kind of Indian and never any of our kind.

The man, Mr. Lal Ravinder, or maybe his name was the other way around, wear a tight suit with a collar fit to choke him. His face look like it been waxed, and his cheeks puff out, maybe because of his tight shirt.

I explain the whole story to him, right from the time Old Joe died.

He looked puzzled at me for a long time, then he smile real bright.

"Did you do work on the farm?"

"Yes, sure, I did lots of chores for Old Joe the last few years."

"Did he pay you, please?" say the varnish-faced Indian.

"No."

"Oh, then you are entitled to compensation for your work done," and he smile like someone just showed him what sex was all about. "You can file a claim for compensation against the estate…"

"I don't want to be paid for *that* work. I done that because Joe was my friend. You don't file a claim for work done for love."

"You would be able to claim for services rendered, please," he insist.

"That's not what I asked about," I explain. "I'm not owed wages."

"Then you must get one of his relatives to come in and talk to us."

I feel like I'm staring in one of them funny mirrors at the Calgary Stampede midway. This fellow ain't understood anything I've said to him.

"HE HAS NO RELATIVES," I yell.

"Not to speak harshly, please."

Mad Etta rumble up to the counter.

"You know what a lawyer is?" she ask that Indian, whose eyes get big when he see the size of Etta.

"Oh, yes please," say Mr. Lal.

"Well in Indian country I'm a lawyer, and I fry three small fish like you for breakfast every day. So bring me your boss—real quick, please."

That little fellow scuttle away.

Pretty soon two big men with bald heads and necks like turkeys come and talk with us. We have to tell our story all over again. They are more civil, but they say rules is rules and they don't recognize no Indian law. If Joe didn't leave the land and money to me, in writing, then it look like it gonna belong to the Government.

What the Government will do, they say, is to pay off Joe's debts from his money in his bank, then they put up the farm, buildings and equipment, for sale by tender, whatever that mean—and if that don't work they sell the farm by a real estate man. All the money they get go to the Government, be buried forever in some dark place.

We is sure sad when we leave there.

Later on, down at the Indian Friendship Centre in Edmonton, Dave Smallface give me the card of a lawyer who been around saying he like to help out us Indians.

His office is in a real old building downtown, and the elevator grunt and groan its way up with me and Mad Etta inside. The glass in his office door is ice coloured and rough as a carrot grater. His name is printed in black behind that ice: Edward J. Shadbolt, BA, LLB.

Mr. Shadbolt ain't been in business very long, and we can still smell sawdust in his office and see where partitions been moved around. A bell tingles when we open the outside door and Mr. Shadbolt himself come out to meet us, say he ain't even hired a secretary yet. He be awful young for a lawyer, have wide spaced eyes and an expression on his face like he just stuck his head through a curtain to surprise somebody.

I tell him my whole story. By this time I am getting tired of telling it.

"You're sure there isn't anything in writing, a letter perhaps, something where Mr. Buffalo might have just mentioned his wish to have the farm go to you?"

"Old Joe could only write his name. The letters didn't mean nothing to him. He only copied what somebody showed him was his name," I say, hoping that this guy at least understood and won't make me go over the story again.

"Don't need no letters," say Etta. "Joe Buffalo told *me*. That's how it was done in the old days. If your family was gone, your chief or your medicine man look after things like that. The land was to go to Silas here, along with half his money. The other half of the money was to go to the Catholic church in his dead daughter's name. Not because Old Joe liked the church but because she did, and he loved her a lot."

"Did you write down his request? Did he sign it?"

"No need," say Etta. "I got a memory like an otter trap. I remember the whole thing. I just told you."

The lawyer made a bad face.

"I have no legal argument," he say. "Verbal agreements hold no water with a court. So unless you can come up with some documents…" and his voice faded away like turning down the volume on a radio.

"How about Indian law?" asks Etta. "Silas here read somewheres that they recognize medicine men as regular doctors—must be the same with lawyers. What do you know about that?"

The lawyer shake his head. "I don't know anything about Indian Law; if there is such a thing it is not recognized by the Canadian courts."

We all sit silent for a minute. Then the lawyer's face get to look like it have an idea behind it.

"Tell me about your family, Silas," he say, and I do, and he ask a lot of questions about how old everybody is, especially my mother.

"The only thing I can think of that we might be able to do," he say, "would be if we could get your mother to sign a statement saying that Old Joe Buffalo was your real father. Then you would be entitled to inherit his estate."

"My father was still living at home back then," I say. "Old Joe wouldn't mess with a married woman, and my mother…"

"I'm not suggesting he did," says Mr. Shadbolt, "but it would be a way for you to get what is rightfully yours."

"I don't want it that bad," I say.

"It was just an idea," he say. "I didn't think you people were so particular about that sort of thing."

Outside, while I'm shoving Etta into the back of a taxi,

I get an idea of my own. I tell Etta and she allow as it is a pretty good one. Etta is always for having other people do your work for you if you can arrange it.

We look up the offices of the Catholic Church, go there and tell them how this nice old man want to leave them $20,000 but the Government say it going to take all that money for itself. "The more money people got, the more they like to get," say Mad Etta after we is outside, loaded down with promises that they look into the case real thorough. "Ain't nobody I ever met as rich or greedy as the Catholic Church," say Etta, "so we can be sure they'll do everything they can to get more. And if they help us on the way, well…" and she smile right around to the back of her neck.

Joe's farm just sit vacant all summer and fall. The hollyhocks are tall in front of the window and the yard grow a carpet of chickweed and creeping charlie, with big stocks of lambsquarter sticking up like trees. I figure it all been forgot about when me and Etta, and Sadie all get big, fat registered letters, full of legal looking papers say we got to go to court in Edmonton on a certain date.

The Church don't have just one lawyer, they got four, all dressed like the dummies in the window of the Tip-Top Tailors store in Wetaskiwin. The two old lawyers each have a young lawyer just to carry their books and briefcases.

The trial take place in a little, tiny courtroom, and it is called a civil case of Archdiocese of Edmonton vs. Government of Alberta. It sure ain't exciting. I understand English pretty good, but they might as well be talking German or Polish for all I can make of it. We all get to tell our stories over and over. Finally, they tell us to go home, that the judge is going to reserve his decisions, whatever that mean. I should have my friend Frank Fence-post there; he could make some jokes about reserve decisions.

Across the highway from the reserve, where Old Joe's

land is—and for a long way both east and south—the
farms is all owned by a company, not by local farmers.

A year or so ago me and Frank Fence-post was driving
a side-road when we seen a little concrete-block building
off in a wheat field on one of them company farms.
There was a pickup truck beside the building so we drove
in and the man there take us inside. There was no
windows, just a tiny desk lamp and bluish light from a
television set—only it didn't show regular TV shows like
Dallas, but was what the man called "closed circuit."
Over in the corner was a machine with red and green
flashing lights, look like the inside of an airplane I seen
once.

The man tells us that he run 10,000 acres of wheat
farm from that concrete box. The TV tell him all he
needs to know about weather, planting, spraying and
harvesting. And if he want anything else he just have to
punch in numbers on that machine, what he called a
"green thumb box."

Why from right there that man, pale and weak looking
as he was, could send out combines to gobble up the
wheat, spit it into trucks and send it off to market.

"You're kind of like God, ain't you?" says Frank.

The man nod.

"Could you make it rain, partner?" I asked. He only
smiled, but I bet he could of.

And it is those people, called computer farmers, who
buy Old Joe's place. I guess the Government, when it
make up its mind, can be even tougher than the Catholic
Church.

Nobody cares. And it makes me awful mad. It all been
decided by white men who don't know nothing about an
old man's mind. It ain't right that they can take away
for themselves what was supposed to be mine. But who
do I fight? It's like I been tossed in water where I can
watch myself drown but can't move to stop it.

"Boy, you're crazy," is what Frank say to me when I

tell him what I'm gonna do. "But you know me, I like to help you do crazy things," and he slap my back and give me a punch on the arm.

Frank Fence-post has this here gift—he is able to open most locks just by looking at them, or at least by twisting a piece of wire, or tinfoil off a cigarette package.

Late in the night we drive a few miles south and a few miles west to where a road construction crew is working. It is that time after the first frost and before the snow, what people call Indian Summer. The sky is clear and frost make the grain stubble look like white whiskers. There ain't no farm houses around and the construction equipment stand silent in the moonlight, look big and scary as dinosaurs. I pull Louis Coyote's pickup truck off the road and turn off the lights.

"Which one do you want?" says Frank.

I pick one that got wheels taller than me, and a big scraper on the front of it.

Frank climb up on it, looks small as a little boy. In a minute there is a roar loud as an earthquake in a junk-yard as the machine come to life. Frank turn on its light and the beam must shoot a hundred yards ahead, look like it shining from the top of a bridge.

Frank show me how to shift the gears so's I can drive it.

"I'll follow a mile or so behind. If the RCMP's come along you can run cross-country to the next section-line road and I'll pick you up there."

It is about ten miles to Old Joe's place. I feel like I'm riding a ferris wheel as I drive along the gravel road, and then on Highway 2A up towards Hobbema. At Joe's I don't bother opening the gate, just run straight over it making the posts crack, and the barbed wire zing through the air, staples screaming like shot rabbits, as they pull out of the tamarack posts.

I stop in front of Joe's cabin and take one last look at it there in the moonlight, then drive right into it, as far as the machine will go—back up and ram it again—that cabin break up like it was made of balsa-wood. In ten minutes I got it flat and scattered across the yard like bones been picked by wolves. After that I knock down the corral fence, the small barn and the two granaries.

Then I let my machine straddle the fence and I take it down each way to the end of the quarter section. Finally, I shut the machine off and walk out to the highway— way off in the bluey distance I can see the weak lights of Louis' pickup as Frank comes to take me home.

When that big company take over the land, I want them to find it empty. And except that the buffalo be gone, as wild, and open, and lifeless, as it was when Old Joe first seen it nearly a hundred years ago.

WHERE THE
WILD THINGS
ARE

ME AND MY friend Frank Fence-post we is walking down
the main street of this town called Rocky Mountain
House. We is laughing and taking turns pushing each
other off the sidewalk and into the gutter, when this big,
long car pull up beside us. Boy, you don't even have to
see who's driving to tell it is owned by rich people. It is
one of these Chrysler Imperials, the colour of thick cream,
and it been shined to within an inch of its life. There is a
polite little whirr as the power window on the passenger
side slide down. A man with a square red face, wearing a
scarlet duck-hunter's vest, stick his head out.

"Can y'all tell us where we can find a good hunting
guide?" the man says. I already peeked at the front of the
car and seen that it is from a foreign country called
Alabama.

Frank, he first stop laughing, then he turn his back on
the guy in the car for about three seconds. As Frank turn
around he straighten up, look about seven foot tall.

"You are in luck, white man," Frank say slow and
clear. "I am Fence-post, chief of the Onagotchies. We are
mountain people, all born to hunt and to guide." Frank
keep his shoulders back and stare down on the guy who
is looking out the car window.

I have to turn away to keep from laughing. I've seen Frank do this before. Trouble is he never remember what tribe he say he comes from.

"No kiddin', you guys are really guides?" say the man.

"An Onagoochie does not lie," says Frank, raising up his right hand as if he was a traffic cop.

"Well, listen, we got our licences and everything but the law says we can't go out without a guide. And the guy who sold us the licence says most of the guides are booked up.

"Once again you are in luck, white man. My friend, Standing-Silent-in-Running-Water and I have just finished guiding the famous Duke of Camrose for two weeks. But I warn you we is expensive." Frank slap his right hand across his heart and stare even harder at the man.

"Well, money we got but a guide we ain't. Consider yourself hired. Right Cal?" says the man at the window. The man driving, who is lean and wearing a cowboy hat that touch the roof, nod his agreement.

I'm just standing by the front fender getting ready to run soon as Frank finishes his joke. I mean we hunt gophers with a 22 rifle, and once in a while we shoot a partridge and bring it home, but neither of us like to clean it and even if Ma does cook it up it don't taste nearly as good as Kentucky Fried Chicken.

"Cost you $2000 for a week. Genuine Onadatchie guides do not come cheap."

From where I am I can see both guys take deep breaths.

"Right," they say together. "We want you to take us where the wild things are."

"Five hundred in advance," says Frank, stand and look solemn.

They is both silent for a minute. Then the guy at the window say, "Hop in the back. We'll stop at the hotel and get you the money."

I expect Frank to break and run, but instead he open

the back door and disappear into the car. Then his own window buzz down and he crook his hand for me to come closer.

"Come here, Standing-Silent-in-Running-Water," he says.

"Call me Si," I say.

"Good assistants are hard to come by," Frank says real loud. "Listen, Standing-in-Running-Water, I want you should go and visit our friend and fellow Onagatchie, Verne Gauthier. I will meet you after I have finished my business."

I go to say something but Frank looks mean at me and says, "I have spoken."

"Right, Chief," I say and give him the traffic cop sign.

Frank winks at me as the window whir up and the car glide away from the curb. I know exactly what Frank is talking about. We got a good friend here in Rocky Mountain House, name of Verne Gauthier, who really be a hunting guide. I know enough to go over to Verne's and wait for Frank. Frank must be planning just to grab the money and run. I sure ain't in the mood for no hunting trip, even if the pay is good.

Frank, when he talking to them hunters be talking the way Verne Gauthier teached us. "Hey, don't you never tell my old lady I said this, but guiding is about 90% babysitting. What other babysitter you know makes a thousand bucks a week?" It is Verne who tell us, "When you're talking to hunters always make like you learned English from listening to Tonto on the TV. That way they figure they got the real thing for a guide. I never let a hunter know I been for one year to the university. Another guide out here, he writes poetry, even had some of it printed up, but he never lets on when he's working. These Americans always have trouble with my name, so I just tell 'em, 'Call me Goat,' and they do. Makes me sound tough. You always got to keep an advantage over these guys."

I amble over to Verne Gauthier's place which be about

a mile outside of town. Verne got what he call a lodge, but is really just a glorified bunkhouse. Verne look like a guide is supposed to. He is slim, got a cowboy hat low over his eyes, wear a leather vest, faded Levi's and boots. His face is weathered, his jaw square and he squint up one of his eyes when he talks.

"You guys don't have licence, get in plenty trouble if you work as guides."

"Hey, this is me, Silas, you don't have to talk that way."

"Sorry," says Verne. "I forgot who I was talking to." He laugh when I tell him how Frank got us the job. "I'll loan you horses if you need them and you can have some of my equipment if me or my men ain't using it. That Fence-post, he's gonna be Prime Minister one of these days."

As we talk, two vehicles pull into the yard: that mile-long Chrysler and a safari truck that looks stuffed to the gills with every kind of equipment you can imagine.

Frank grinning out from the window of that Chrysler, and it easy to see he stopped off at a store and spent some of our advance money. Instead of his green John Deere cap he got on a black felt ten-gallon hat with an orange head-band and a green feather wave up over the top. And he bought himself a thick orange blanket that he wrapped around himself.

"What we got here is Fence-post, Chief of the Onago-chies," I say to Verne.

"I'll buy that," he says, and walks over to the car. "How," he says to the guy staring out the driver's window.

"How," says Frank knocking off his hat as he climb out of the back. Instead of running shoes Frank now wearing beaded moccasins that come up most to his knees.

I introduce Verne to the two hunters, Cal is one and Bobo's the other.

"Call me Goat," says Verne, shaking hands very solemn-like. "Welcome to my lodge. I have one room left." Then he quote a price about twice as much as I know he let rooms for.

Cal and Bobo decide to take it. It really funny, but what they getting ain't half as nice as the Rocky Mountain House Hotel where they already got a room. It be that word lodge, and us Indians, is what make them decide.

"You are wise men," Verne says to the hunters. "You have hired the best guides. Goat will give you his best room. Very brave guide you have," he say pointing to Frank. "Us Indians call him Kills-Many-Bears-Without-Fear, but he prefer more modest name of Fence-post, Chief of the Ona..."

"Onadatchies," says Frank.

"Onagotchies," I say.

"Very brave," says Verne, and though his face is straight, I can tell his chest is laughing by the way he breathes.

Bobo, who is tall and lean and wearing blue-tinted glasses and about a thousand dollars worth of hunting clothes, is an accountant. Cal says he is a stock broker, but when I tell him my papa one time work at Weiller and Williams Stockyards in Edmonton, he only laugh.

"Are there really bears around here?" ask Cal.

"Have no fear," says Frank. "You have bravest guide in all of North West Territories, me," and he beat his fists on his chest.

"Ah thought we were in Alberta," says Bobo.

"That too," says Frank. "Now, dawn is the best time for hunting. Be ready one hour before dawn. Me and Standing-Kneedeep-in-Dirty-Water here will meet you. In the meantime you won't mind if we take the safari truck and collect our own supplies."

The hunters look at Verne. He nods that it is okay.

"Never tell these suckers anything they don't need to

know," Verne says to us in Cree. "Always sound solemn, and never let on you're in trouble, even if you're hanging by one hand from a cliff and a grizzly bear is snapping at your ass." Then to the hunters he say, "Goat fry venison steak for supper. Very good." He makes smacking sounds with his lips.

The hunters smile and nod. "You have firewater?" he says to them. They nod again. "Bring inside. At Goat's you not only learn how to hunt, you learn how to drink."

Boy, that safari truck got about twelve gears and more than one of them is reverse, but once I get it up over 90 it stay there pretty good. We head back to Hobbema, get our girls; Connie Bigcharles is Frank's, Sadie Onewound is mine, and we head to the Alice Hotel in Wetaskiwin where we have us a real party with the money Frank got as an advance. Good thing the sun get up late this time of year because it is morning already when we get back to Verne's lodge. Our hunters look a little worse for wear so we have time to drink a cup of coffee with them before we head out.

"Where is your equipment?" is the first thing Bobo the accountant want to know.

"You got so much stuff here, partner, it didn't look like there was room for nothing more," I say, thinking real quick. Actually we was at least gonna get some sleeping bags and borrow some field glasses, but we forgot because we was making such a good party.

"Us Onagotchies live off the land," says Frank, acting like he is insulted by the question.

"You really know your way around this country?" says the accountant, staring at the miles and miles of dark timber that be all around us.

"Know this land like the inside of my mouth," says Frank.

The hunters nod, but I notice one of them is looking at the spot in Frank's face where he have a couple of teeth knocked out in a fight at the Alice Hotel bar.

The morning is misty and a mean little wind saw at us as we walk through tangled brush and over fallen trees to get to a ridge where we have a view of a wide valley.

"That wind is really cold," says Bobo, scrunching up his shoulders, "and strong too."

"Keep eyes on sky," says Frank. "You only have to worry when you see a dead elk drifting by."

For once a white man recognize a joke. "You got a good sense of humour," Cal says.

"Goes with the territory," says Frank. "A Chief got to be smarter, braver, quicker...LOOK OUT A DEAD ELK," he yell and dive into a pile of brown leaves.

"I thought we were supposed to be quiet," says Bobo, who is lugging his rifle and about three hundred pounds of equipment, all look to be brand new.

"Not this close to the lodge," says Frank. "I just trying to get you guys warmed up. Did you know it get so cold out here in the winter we have to jump-start the wolves? Ain't that right, Standing-Upright-in-a-Wet-River?"

"Call me Si," I say, trying to keep a straight face.

All last evening and even this morning I try to talk Frank out of taking this job. I argue that we could head back to the reserve with what left of that $500 and be rich Indians for a week or so. But Frank he got his eye on that other $1500 and he figure it be easy to earn.

"Hey, there's so much game in the mountains we just take them up there and they bound to shoot something."

"But we don't know nothing about being guides."

"You never hear of on-the-job-training?" says Frank, grin from under that big black hat of his.

I remember Verne telling us that the hardest part of being a guide is finding things to keep the hunters busy all day.

"Ninety percent of your hunting is done at dawn and dusk, but there is one long time in between. If you play it smart you let your hunters do the work and you rest up," Verne told us.

I am sure anxious for some rest because me and Frank ain't been asleep yet since yesterday.

We get to the top of a ridge where there is a view of a wide valley. "You guys take out your binoculars," I tell the hunters, "make yourselves comfortable by lying down in the leaves and then you 'glass' the opposite hills there, real slow and careful, see if you can't find us some elk or deer or even a moose. Me and the Chief we go down the ridge a ways and do the same."

"Don't you have glasses?" Cal wants to know.

"Onahatchies have eyes quicker than eagles," says Frank, squinting up his face. "Look off at far mountain! See patch of blue timber half way up? See log in front of blue timber? There are three squirrels sit in a row on that log."

The hunters are quick to get their glasses out of their cases. What the hunters don't know that we do, is that the animals all been out to eat at dawn and we ain't likely to see them again until dusk. But glassing the mountains give those hunters something to do. Me and Frank we drag an air-mattress out of the safari truck and we set it up about a hundred yards from Cal and Bobo. We lay down, prop our heads on our arms like we was staring across at the timber and we asleep before you can count to ten. The mist has lifted, the sun is warm and boy do we have us a good sleep for a couple of hours.

We never see no game that day or the next and our hunters, who say they have never been big game hunting before, are getting a little nervous. The third day we talk Verne into loaning us each a horse. That way we can go higher and deeper into the forest, have more chance of finding something to shoot at. We also decide, that if we don't shoot no game by dusk, that we camp overnight.

The hunters, ain't as dumb as we would of expected, they do know the front end of a horse from the back. Which is about all Frank and me know. The hunters assume we know all about handling and loading and riding horses and we have to pretend that we do.

"You guys are a lot happier with horses than with a car, eh?" says Bobo.

"Oh, yeah, we sure do like these here horses," we say.

Guess they figure we must of rode pinto ponies bare-back and all that stuff they seen in movies. Me and Frank I bet ain't been on a horse more than ten times in our lives. And then we rode a couple of sway-backed greys belong to Louis Coyote and must be twenty years old. One time, on a dare, I enter the bucking horse event at the Rimbey Rodeo. I stay on that horse all of three seconds, land right on my face in the dust, limp and be dizzy for about two weeks.

These here horses of Verne's sure ain't twenty years old, and they don't stand still so good even when you tell them to. Cal and Bobo know how to ride horses and they tie their gear on a lot better than we do, even though I watch them and try to do what they do.

We push on up the mountain, Frank in the lead and me bringing up the rear. We getting to high country, where the timber is thinner and so is the air, when about the worst thing that can happen does. Frank's horse step right down on a hornet's nest. The hornets rise up, look like big gold flies in the sunlight and they start right in to bite both Frank and his horse.

Well that horse dance along the edge of the path, buck a few times like it is used to working the Calgary Stampede Rodeo. Frank he yell like he been murdered. It hard to tell how far down it is because the brush and vines is mighty thick at the side of the trail. Cal and Bobo stopped and they is turning their horses around. There is hornets buzzing all through the air. One must bite my horse because he all of a sudden start running backwards and sideways. Out of the corner of my eye I see Frank's horse turn its belly toward the sun and send Frank off over the cliff in a blur of orange blanket and a loud yell.

I wave my arms around and grab onto a sapling as we going by. Guess I didn't fasten the cinch up tight enough because the saddle start to slip down the side of the horse and I slip down with it. Pretty soon the saddle is on the underside of the horse and I am too. I hang onto the saddle-horn and if I scrunch up, my head just misses the ground. That horse is dancing in circles for a while and then I feel him running pretty fast. I sure do feel silly, stuck upside down the way I am, but I ain't about to let go 'cause the ground is hard and the horse's hooves even harder.

Finally, I hear Bobo's voice talking soft to my horse and then I can see Bobo's legs and from the position he is in I guess that he got a hold of the reins.

"You can let go now, Si," he says.

Boy, I is some scratched up from riding with my nose so close to the ground, and I sure do feel foolish to be rescued by one of the men we supposed to be guiding. Bobo look at me like a school teacher just caught me with answers written on my hand.

"Where's Frank?" I ask.

"How much experience have you guys had as guides?" asks Bobo. He is fingering a hornet bite on the side of his nose.

"I ain't had that much," I say. I discover I got about six hornet bites on me, some in places I would never expect a hornet to get to. "I'm just the assistant. Chief Fence-post he's the expert guide."

"Some expert," says Cal, retying his gear behind his saddle.

Just then Frank come crashing out of the forest from behind us. His blanket be full of blackberry canes and his face look like it be been locked up in a bag full of cats.

"Onadatchies have the blood of ravens in their veins," he say. "First you see us one place then we all of a sudden in another," and he nod his head up and down try to smile.

"Onagotchies," I whisper.

"Whatever," says Frank.

"Well, Fence-post," says Bobo. "Last we saw of your horse it was heading down the mountain about ninety miles an hour. You're going to have to double with one of us."

"Boy, if this day was a fish, I'd throw it back," says Frank, kind of resting his head on my shoulder. Then we head back to Verne's lodge.

"How much hunting have you guys done?" I ask Cal and Bobo at supper that evening.

"We're no greenhorns," says Bobo.

"But how much?"

"A few quail back home," says Cal.

"And possum," says Bobo.

"Don't worry about us. We won't get buck fever. Just find us some of these here big game animals, if you can."

"Hey, Chief," Bobo says, changing the subject, "how come you never say the name of your tribe the same two times in a row? And I never heard of a tribe with a name like yours, and I got a map from the tourist bureau showing where all the Indian tribes live."

"Onagotchies are kind of like the Cree," I say.

Everybody look over at Frank for the answer.

"The Great Spirit speak with many tongues. Pass the beans," says Frank.

"Hey," say Cal in a loud whisper, "I see something." It is next morning and we got the hunters glassing the mountain again. Bobo is busy getting his glasses on the same line as Cal's. Frank put his hand over his eyes to use as a visor and pretend he sees what they see.

"Moose, deer, goats," they is saying.

I borrow Cal's glasses and take a look where he is pointing. Sure enough, across a small valley and up about 500 feet there are maybe a half-dozen elk moving in and out among the trees.

We try to move fast and quiet, down the hill, across a meadow and back up into the timber. When we get to a spot I figure is close to them elk, but still over a hill from them, I have everyone stop.

When we stand silent we can hear from over the hill the sound of twigs cracking. Cal and Bobo get their guns all ready to fire. They start to creep forward but I signal them to stay put.

Verne Gauthier has loaned me an elk-bugle. "This was made by a real Indian," he say to me, "carved from a moose-bone." It is about four inches long, shiny-smooth, and got little holes drilled in it. "You blow on it like it was a mouth-organ," Verne said, and he showed me quite a few times how to make the right kind of call on it.

I take a deep breath and blow into that elk-bugle just the way Verne showed me. The sound come out in three loud whistles and then a lower note that hang in the air for a while. About ten seconds after that last note die away, there is a terrific crashing from over the hill and when we look up a big bull elk stand at the crest of the hill staring down at us.

What happen then make me feel like I'm standing in a park full of statues. I bet all four of us stare at the elk and the elk stare back for maybe five seconds. Frank is froze in a position with his arms raised under his blanket, make him look like an orange bat doing a ceremony of some kind. Finally, there is a bunch of shots, but I can see right away that instead of shoot the elk, Bobo has emptied his gun straight into the ground in front of his feet. The elk whirl and is gone while the shots still echoing. Cal still stare straight ahead his gun cradled in his arm as if it was a piece of wood. I don't have a gun but I was at least *thinking* about shooting that elk.

"Hey, Frank," I say, pulling on one of his arms.

"Don't speak to your Chief by his slave name," he says. "I am Fence-post, Chief of the Onagotchies!"

"I think you're beginning to believe that stuff."

"What's to believe? One inherits the blood of a Chief."

Bobo and Cal standing with their heads bowed, look like they been attending a funeral. Far off, I can hear the elk crashing through the timber.

We don't see no game for the rest of the day and that night we camp out. Cal and Bobo have more equipment than they ever gonna need but they believe Frank when he tell them us Indians live off the land. White men don't seem to understand that Indians get as cold, as wet, and need as much sleep as they do.

When we see they ain't about to share their bedrolls, why Frank he start in to tell stories. The stories all be about hunters who got chased and ate by bears while they camping out in the dark in the mountains.

"Lost two hunters just over a month ago," he say real serious. "Very sad. I offer to drive the bears away for a mere $100 each, but they did not believe in the powers of Fence-post, Chief of the Onodatchies."

"What ya'll do to keep bears away?" says Cal.

"Some roots and leaves, when boiled a certain way are most unpleasant to bears. I boil up medicine, pour it in a circle around the camp. Bears *never* cross over that line."

Cal and Bobo ain't quick to part with more money so Frank tell another story about finding parts of hunters scattered over a half-mile area. "Just like a plane crash," he say and look real sad. "But if you short of cash for only $50 I put the evil eye on the bears," says Frank. Then he stand up, fold his arms across his chest and turn slowly around, staring mean at the forest.

"Does that really work?" asks Bobo.

"Do you see any bears?" answers Frank.

The later the time and the lower the fire the more nervous Cal and Bobo get. Everytime a mouse move in the underbrush they jump about two feet each.

Finally, they get together and offer Frank a hundred dollars total to make up his medicine. Verne Gauthier is right, one day Frank going to be the Prime Minister, if he lives long enough. Our class at the Tech School voted Frank the student most likely to get murdered.

Frank he go away from the light of the camp fire, pick

some roots and leaves—I imagine he get the first ones he
come to because Frank he is as afraid of bears as anybody. Bears is something real guides have to worry
about all the time, but the answer is to pick a high
campsite and keep a rifle close by. Frank boil up that
stuff in a kettle and then he disappear again into the
forest. We is camped on a high knoll with a sharp drop
on one side, so all Frank have to do is pour his medicine
in a semi-circle around the camp.

Boy, we all jump some when we hear Frank scream. It
scare me too because I know it is a real scream and not
Frank trying to earn his money. Right after the scream
comes sounds like two buffalo wrestling in the timber
and Frank charge though the camp yelling "Bears!
Bears!" and dive over the edge of the embankment. Then
we hear the blackberry vines crackle and Frank yell
some more.

Cal and Bobo was already in their sleeping bags with
only their heads sticking out of their pup tent. First they
stand half-way up in their sleeping bags, then they fall
down take the tent with them. Together they manage to
drag the whole mess over the side of the mountain, all
the time yelling like they was being tortured.

The first thing I done was grab Bobo's rifle. I'm scared
of bears too, but if there was a bear chasing Frank it
should of been right on his tail. I slide over the edge of the
cliff, brace my feet on a rock and the rifle on my shoulder.
I figure if a bear is coming I get off three quick shots and
then throw myself backwards into whatever is down
there. I can hear Frank and Cal and Bobo, crashing and
cursing and yelling somewhere in the dark below me.

I wait for a long time and when there still ain't no sign
of a bear I stand up and walk careful across the camp
toward the place Frank come from. The trees make long
shadows everywhere and it sure is scary. About twenty-
five feet into the forest I see a broken pine branch hanging down and in the shadows it look just like a bear's

arm. I bet Frank walked under it and it scratched the back of his neck. I fire three shots in the air and scuff some deadfall around. I'll tell them I scared the bear away, maybe even wounded it. I don't think Cal and Bobo would want to know the truth.

In the morning everybody but me is stiff and sore and scratched up pretty good. Frank is limping like he been kicked by a horse. He don't seem to mind if I call him Frank and he ain't called me Standing-in-Running-Water-up-to-his-Neck yet today. Cal and Bobo, and even Frank who really thought there was a bear after him, are nice to me for being brave and scaring off the bear.

We left the safari truck way at the bottom of a long slope. When I get down there with an armload of equipment I feeling so happy I figure it be easy to drive the truck right up to the top where the campsite is. It sure be easier than carrying all the stuff down, especially since I is the only one healthy enough to carry equipment this morning. In daylight the trees look a lot further apart than they did at dusk. The truck is facing down the mountain and since there ain't no place to turn around I decide to back it up to the camp. There is about three reverse gears in the truck and I put it in what I figure to be the lowest, and the truck creep backward across the pine-needle floor of the forest. It crawl along just like one of these here battery-powered toys I buy for my brothers, Hiram, Thomas, and Joseph.

I smiling pretty good when I get to the top. Everybody is sure happy not to have to carry the gear down the mountain, especially me.

I hop out and am just about to start loading stuff when I realize something ain't right. There must of been one more reverse gear than I figured because the truck is still creeping backward and is awful close to the edge.

Cal and Bobo even got buck fever when it come to the truck. They just stand and watch, their eyes getting bigger and bigger. They can't even find their voices to yell. As I turn toward the truck I get one quick view all the way down to the valley where a river roars along full of black rocks and white water. I figure that even if it kills me I better stick with the truck. I take a run and dive at the open driver's window, but I only about half-way in when the truck go over the first ledge. We drop maybe ten feet and land in the blackberry vines. The vines bend way down and the truck settle soft as a feather. I'm almost all inside when I feel them years and years worth of vines spring us back up. We just keep rising like we was on a fork-lift until the truck hurtle off into space and I figure I'm a goner for sure. But the second ledge is only down twenty feet or so and is grassy and sunny and what surprise me most, full of elk. It must only take a second or so for us to fall but it seem like a full minute until the truck land, kind of sideways and right on an elk what was trying to get away. That truck squash the elk like it was a rabbit on the highway, roll sideways and bounce down the rough rock hill to the river. I feel like the time Frank Fence-post rolled me down a long hill inside an oil barrel. I shake my head and find myself sitting on the white gravel near the edge of the water.

As I watch, that safari truck grind out into the river. I follow for a few steps but the water is too cold for me to go in over my boots. Pretty soon the current catch up the truck, lift its wheels off the gravel, swing it sideways and off it go down the river.

I can hear Cal and Bobo and Fence-post, Chief of the Onagotchies, crashing through the timber on the side of the hill. I hope Cal and Bobo ain't gonna be too mad. I mean after all I have killed them an elk and that was what they come for.

DR. DON

"How come you don't mind?" I ask Mad Etta our medicine lady.

"Hey, when you're young like you, Silas, you don't like nobody move in on your territory. But when you get old as me, you look forward to all the help you can get."

Who and what I been asking about is Dr. Don. His whole name is Dr. Donald Morninglight. He is an Indian and a doctor who come to the reserve about three months ago.

"He ain't as good as me. Never will be," say Mad Etta, as she laugh and laugh, shake on the tree-trunk chair in her cabin.

Must be ten years since we had a full time doctor here on the Ermineskin Reserve. Maybe three times a year the Department of Indian Affairs doctors come around but they is all white and wear coats white as bathroom fixtures, smell of disinfectant, and to see them work remind me of a film I seen of assembly line workers who put cars together. Them doctors treat people as if they was cars need a new bolt or screw to be whole again.

But Dr. Don don't be like that. Guess being an Indian helps. One reason we never been able to keep a doctor

here is they never like to live on the reserve. Even Indian
Affairs can't get for them a fancy enough place to live.
But Dr. Don when he come, just move into a vacant
house near to Blue Quills Hall. He don't act like doctors
we know, except that he make sick people better, and, as
I say, even Mad Etta like him. And you got to be liked by
Mad Etta if you is to get any respect around the reserve.

"Dr. Don he know which side his medical practice be
buttered on," says my friend Frank Fence-post. And I
guess Frank is right. Quite a few times in the first month
Dr. Don was here, he come over to Etta's place in the
evening, have a beer with her and tell her about patients
he having trouble curing. Etta give him her advice. I
don't know if he ever take it but it sure make Etta feel
good. So good, that right now she would do just about
anything for Dr. Don.

It is easy to tell by looking at Dr. Don that he is some
kind of Indian. But he never say which kind.

"I'm a mongrel," he say when asked, and laugh. "If
you went far enough back you'd find Cree blood in me."

Dr. Don ain't a handsome man at all. He is about 40,
got short legs and a little pot belly. His hair be thin on
top and what he got stand out like it never seen a comb.
His eyes is dark and deep-set, his nose too big, and he got
a thick black moustache that droop over his top lip. But
he got such a friendly way about him that everybody
like him. He ask a lot of questions and he already know
how to make a good try at speaking Cree.

His wife is named Paula. She is an Indian, too, and as
shy as anything. She have a new baby the doctor say is
called Morning After Rain. I think it was a girl.

He only been here, I bet a month, when I see him
walking across the reserve with Chief Tom. At least
Chief Tom is walking, taking long steps with his head
down. Dr. Don have to almost dance to keep up with
him, and to get a bit in front so he can talk to his face.

I'm a long way behind them, but the words carry in
the cold air. From Dr. Don I hear words like clinic,

Government Grants, nurse, disgrace, and about ten times, money.

Chief Tom only shake his head. We all know the Chief, being a Government MLA, could do lots of things for us if he really wanted. But he is more interested in sell off timber or give away land to make himself look good to the white people.

It don't take Dr. Don long to spot him for what he is.

"When is the next election for Chief?" he ask us.

"Next summer," we tell him.

"We'd better get an organization started soon. That Chief of yours needs to be replaced and fast."

We suggest he should run.

"Hey, I'm Indian, but not Cree. How about a woman Chief? Bedelia Coyote isn't afraid of anyone, and she's a very knowledgable young woman where Indian problems are concerned."

Some of us get working on that right away.

I sure hope Dr. Don knows what he is doing. Chief Tom be a dangerous man to have as an enemy, 'cause he know lots of white people in high places.

At Christmas time, Dr. Don he stay right on the reserve. All the doctors in Wetaskiwin and Ponoka run off to Hawaii or someplace hot, but Dr. Don just pitch in and act like he is one of us. Funny thing is that a few sick white people who can't find their own doctors come to the reserve to see Dr. Don. Ordinarily, you couldn't get a white man to the reserve with a gun to his head unless he want to convert us to his religion or repossess one of our cars.

On Christmas Eve, Dr. Don emcee the Christmas Concert down to Blue Quills Hall. Boy, he can tell good jokes and everybody have a happy evening.

At the end of the concert he make a little speech to say how happy he and his family is here at Hobbema, and how he plans to work here until he retires and then still stay here.

It make everybody feel all warm inside.

Then he take from his pocket a sheet of paper, and what he read is kind of a poem. I couldn't remember it too good, so I went to see his wife just before her and the baby moved away and she gived it to me. It is the same copy he read at the concert, wrote in blue ink in real tiny handwriting. It seem to me it is both happy and sad at the same time.

> Words are nothing
> like pebbles beside mountains
> Deeds are all that count
> Watch and listen with me this Christmas
> For it is the small daily deeds of men
> that tell the heart what it needs to know
> Quietly, as you have made me welcome
> I will quietly go about my work
> But listen not to my words—wait and watch.

Everybody is silent for about 10 seconds after Dr. Don finish. And, as Frank Fence-post would say, you could have heard a flea fart. Then everybody break into clapping for a long time. Finally, Eli Bird start in soft on his guitar and Mary Boxcar join in on the piano, and we all sing "Silent Night."

One morning in January I meet Dr. Don walk down toward the General Store.

"You ever see anything this beautiful, Silas?" he say, and point at the pinky sky where two pale sundogs hang like grapefruit, one on each side of the sun. It is really cold and Dr. Don's moustache be froze white as if he dipped it in flour.

"That's what I want to be when I die," he say.

"A sundog?"

"A child of the sun—just floating in the morning sky, free as a balloon. Do your people have any legends about sundogs?"

It sure embarrass me but I have to admit I don't know.

"You should write one then," he say.

"Legends aren't really in my line," I say. I sure don't figure that in just a few weeks, I will be writing this story about Dr. Don.

It was Chief Tom's girlfriend, Samantha Yellowknees, who started up the trouble. Chief Tom ain't smart enough to do something like that himself. In fact, if it weren't for Samantha, Chief Tom would still be cutting ties for the railway.

What she done, she tell us one evening at Blue Quills Hall, was to phone the Department of Indian Affairs. "I told them to call the College of Physicians and Surgeons and check out this Dr. Morninglight. There's something not right about him. I can smell a phoney," say Samantha, glare at us, mean as a school teacher.

"If anybody know the smell of a phoney, it be you," says Frank Fence-post. That go right over Chief Tom's head but Samantha look ugly at us and square her chin. Her and Chief Tom been living together for a couple of years in an apartment in Wetaskiwin, ever since the Chief left his wife Mary. Samantha be a city Indian, been to the Toronto University to study sociology.

When we tell Dr. Don what been done he just smile kind of sad and say, "A man should be judged by his deeds." Then he stand silent for a long time.

It was about a week later in the late afternoon that the RCMP car pull up in front of the Residential School where Dr. Don hold his office hours in the Nurse's Room. It is Constable Greer, who be about the only nice RCMP I ever known. Constable Greer got grey hair and sad pouches under his eyes like a dog. But he got with him a young Constable who be about seven feet tall in his fur hat, and speak hardly nothing but French.

Constable Greer read out the charge against Dr. Don, only the name he read don't be Dr. Don's, but three long words that sound like Mexican names you hear on the television. He kind of apologize, but say he got to take Dr. Don to the RCMP office in Wetaskiwin. What he read out say Dr. Don is charged with "Impersonating a Doctor."

Dr. Don finish bandaging up the hand of Caroline Stick. Then he put on his parka and nod to Constable Greer. They is about to walk out when the French Constable step forward, pull out his handcuffs and snap them on Dr. Don's wrists. Then he sort of steer Dr. Don in front of him, look like a giant pushing a child.

Some of us stand around as Dr. Don duck his head and get into the back of the RCMP car. We still stand around even after the car is gone. It is a big shock to all of us. For me it is like that whole place where my stomach is, been empty for a long time.

But the shock is ten times worse the next day when the word come from Wetaskiwin that Dr. Don is dead. Hanged himself with his shirt from the cell bars is what everybody say.

All of a sudden the reserve is crawling with reporters. One of them big trucks from CFRN-TV in Edmonton get up to the school before we tear up the culvert in the road so the rest of them got to walk instead of drive.

Them reporters is kind of angry that we can't tell them anything they don't already know. They are waving a copy of the *Edmonton Journal* with a story that start out:

HOBBEMA—Donato Fernando Tragaluz took his own life after he was unmasked as a medical imposter.

Tragaluz killed himself in the Wetaskiwin RCMP lockup after police arrested him here Tuesday for impersonating a doctor. Using the medical documents of the real Dr. Donald Morninglight, the 42-year-old Tragaluz practised as the town's doctor for nearly four months.

The Journal has learned that Tragaluz posed as a

doctor under several aliases in communities in Canada, the U.S., and Mexico for about ten years, evading medical authorities, police and the FBI.

One group is interviewing Samantha Yellowknees.

"I knew there was something wrong with him," says Samantha, baring her upper teeth like a dog looking at you over a bone. "No real doctor in his right mind would start a practice out here."

"What about his funeral?" they all want to know.

Mrs. Morninglight said she guessed he was Catholic if he was anything. She get some of us to call on the Catholic church, but the priests shy away from the whole deal as if they get germs if they get too close. "He can't be buried by the church because he killed himself," they say. "People who kill themselves is going to hell for sure," is what they say. It seem to me the church do all they can to help them along.

Nobody know what to do for a while. Mrs. Morninglight who always been silent, is even more now. She say she didn't know he wasn't who he said he was. They only been married a little over a year.

"All I want to do is go home," she say. Turn out home for her is South Dakota.

Then Mad Etta step in. Suppose with Mad Etta, I should say waddle. "We got to show we ain't as stupid as the white men, about a lot of things," say Etta and she get me to call a meeting of all the newspaper people who been creep around the reserve on their tip-toes for the last couple of days, take pictures and talk to anybody who even say they knew Dr. Don.

Etta can speak English good as me, but she just sit big as a bear on the tree-trunk chair in her cabin, arms fat as railroad ties folded across her big belly.

"This here is our tribal Medicine Lady," I tell them, squint into the glare of the lights that go with the TV camera. "You ask me questions. I'll translate them to Cree for her. She'll answer in Cree and I'll translate to English for you."

Things are pretty easy at first, except that Mad Etta she leave those easy questions for me to answer. She give a long speech in Cree that the white people think is her answer, but she really be saying things to make me and the other Indians laugh.

Like somebody ask how long she been Medicine Lady.

What she say to me in Cree is, "Look at that guy with the pointed face who ask the question. He got his hair stiffened up like it been mixed with honey. Try to imagine him naked, make love to a woman, or even a goat." She say this real serious.

"Forty-one years," I tell that weasel-faced man.

About two hours before, we buried Dr. Don after having our own service for him at Blue Quills Hall. Take Eathen Firstrider, Robert Coyote, and about a half-dozen other guys all morning to carve out a grave with pickaxes up on a hill where Dr. Don can look down on the town and up at the sky. Mary Boxcar play the piano and we sing the Hank Williams' song, "I've Seen The Light." A few people say nice things about Dr. Don, like Moses Badland, who tell about the time Dr. Don walk eight miles into the bush to sew up the foot he cut while splitting wood.

"He may not have been a real doctor, but at least he show us the kind of medical attention we should expect," say Bedelia Coyote and a few people applaud a bit.

I leave my ski-cap off as me, Eathen, Robert, Frank, Rufus, and Bedelia carry the coffin out of the hall. The wind chew at my ears with its little needle teeth.

"What do you think makes a man do something like that?" one of the reporters ask.

Mad Etta give a real answer to that question.

"Why shouldn't he? Here, if you or anybody else want to call themselves a doctor, it is okay. You just have to find people who trust you to make them better. Maybe he wasn't a doctor, but he had the call. There ain't very many who have the call."

"Then it didn't matter to you that he had never been to university or medical school?"

"People believed in him," growl Mad Etta. "He had the right touch and loving heart. If you like your doctor, you is half-way better. Most sickness is caused by what's between the ears…"

There was sundogs out this morning when we were putting the coffin in the grave, shimmering like peaches there in the cold pink sky. I imagined for a second that I could see Dr. Don's face in one of them, but only for a second.

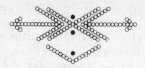

THE COLLEGE

"HEY," SAYS BEDELIA COYOTE as she come bouncing into Blue Quills Hall, "I think I found what I been looking for," and she smile on the group of us that sitting on benches along the wall smoking and resting after play some ping pong.

Bedelia is, quite often to us guys, a pain in the neck. "She was born with a chip on each of her shoulders," my friend Frank Fence-post say about her. Bedelia ain't shy as most Indians: she get the *MS. Magazine* delivered to her and go around calling the other girls sister, even though they ain't related to her. Bedelia is short and stocky and not much good for beautiful, but she got handed out brains instead of good looks.

"I just been up at the Wetaskiwin Library for about five hours. Damn, but it took me an hour of standing out in the wind to thumb a ride home, and then it was two of them creepy students from the Bible College who picked me up. First they laid their Jesus trip on me and when that didn't take, the one who wasn't driving developed about fifteen hands and decided if he couldn't save me he'd fuck me…kept telling me how Indian girls like to have sex with white men." Bedelia stamp her foot hard on the floor, then toss her head to shake back some of the long hair what always fall in her eyes. "They'd of treated me better if they knew what I got written down here," and she unsnap the left pocket of her jean jacket and take out a sheet of loose-leaf refill.

The group of us that sitting around is me, my friend Frank Fence-post, his girl Connie Bigcharles, my girl Sadie One-wound, Rufus Firstrider, David One-wound, Eathen Firstrider and Julie Scar.

"I found out for sure," Bedelia go on, "that the Bible College have a lease with the Tribal Council, signed in 1929 for fifty years at a dollar a year. But this is 1979 and that lease expire soon. They've used fifteen acres of reserve land for fifty years for nothing, and I bet they gonna try to get another lease just like the last one. We got to do something about it." None of us say anything.

"Don't you figure we should do something about it?"

Bedelia is real proud of herself for what she found out and she stand up in front of us with her hands on her hips like she looking for a fight. Still nobody say anything, but we all know from past experience that when Bedelia get mad about something, which is most all of the time, it don't take her long to drag the rest of us into it.

Only a few of us Indians even know that the Brotherhood of the Burning Bush Bible College is located on our reserve here at Hobbema, and most who know don't care one way or another. It was one time at the library in Wetaskiwin while I was looking at history books that Bedelia got out the Township Maps of Alberta and look up on them our Ermineskin Reserve. Them maps all look like pieces of old drafting paper to me and don't interest me much at all but after a while Bedelia come over and pull at the sleeve of my jacket and make me come see what she found.

"Look here, Silas," she says, putting her stubby brown finger down on the map. "That Holy Roller Bible College is on reserve land."

"It do look that way," I say, "but so what?"

"They must be paying somebody rent. I don't ever remember hearing about it."

"Ask Chief Tom," I say. "He's supposed to know all about stuff like that."

"Mr. Yellowknees," say Bedelia, her eyes flashing, "he'd sell the reserve and pocket the money if he was given half a chance." Not many of us young Indians like Chief Tom Crow-eye very much. He wear a shiny blue suit and have his hair styled once a week in a beauty parlour for men.

The Burning Bush Bible College was started a long time ago by some old preacher who was in the Social Credit Government that Alberta had when it was still poor and old fashioned. It be a group of white stucco buildings that surround a red brick church, wide and stocky as a Hereford bull, all set in among lots of green lawns full of flower beds and paved driveways. They be right at the south end of the reserve, have tall chainlink fence all around their grounds and never been very friendly with us Indians. Probably it is because us Indians ain't too much for religion, the white man's kind anyway. I hear that Bible College students, when they graduate have to go to Africa or India or someplace to sign up people for their religion. Guess them other kind of Indians be easier to convert than us.

Religion, to us Indians today, pretty much depend on who's holding the church picnic. Boy, we travel 20-30 miles for free hot dogs, Coke, and ice cream, and we sure promise to come to whatever church giving out that food. We mean it too, at the time, but by the next Sunday our promises be kind of like old newspapers, faded and not much good for anything. One outfit, called Pentecostal Alliance used to send purple school buses out to the reserve real early on Sunday mornings to carry us off to church, got so pushy that we had to remember to tear up the culvert in the road on Saturday nights so they couldn't get up the long hill to our cabins.

White people sure like to have Indians join their religion. It make them feel good to save us from something, I never been sure what, but once they get us signed up they want us to stay out of the way and not dirty up their churches none. I read once a story about Crowfoot the great Indian Chief who was always bothered by white religious men. They all knew how powerful Crowfoot was and figure that if they can convert him why they get all the rest of the Indians in the bargain. Mr. Rev. McDougall, who was I guess a Presbyterian or Methodist, and Father Lacombe the Catholic, was all the time hang around Crowfoot's lodge explain to him over and over how their religion was best and why he should join up with them. Only they each tell a different story, say only their religion is good and the others be bad.

Finally Crowfoot he call Mr. Rev. McDougall and Father Lacombe to his lodge together and he say, "I have decided. I will leave you both in my lodge and you tell your stories to each other. Then after you decide which of you is right, I will join with you and we will all be brothers in the same religion."

They say that after that Crowfoot don't get bothered no more.

It is all a kind of game we play with Bedelia. We ignore her when she want us to get involved with something until she bring up the Ermineskin Warrior Society what was started for us by an American Indian Movement guy who come to the reserve once. Bedelia, like we expect, yell good at us, tell us that we a bunch of old men who got wooden walking sticks instead of peckers; our girlfriends all giggle at that part and Frank Fence-post break in to say he use a telephone pole for a walking stick. Bedelia keep on to tell us that we lazy and no good and let white people walk all over us.

It is about that time that we say, "Well, Bedelia, what is it that you want us to do?"

"What if we was to go down to the Bible College and

talk to them, tell them we can make a lot of trouble if they don't help us some?"

"Like how?" I ask.

"Well, the college use up fifteen acres of our good land. We find out what fifteen acres of farm land rent for and make them pay the same, only the money instead of going to Chief Tom and the tribal council be used for some self-help programmes..." and here Bedelia start listing off figures on alcoholism and drugs, and beat up wives, and suicides, and she go on and on until I'm sorry I asked the question.

We argue for quite a while about whether we should go call on them as we are or if we should act like we figure white peoples expect us to. We finally decide on half and half.

Rufus Firstrider wear only a loin cloth, cover himself with mean paint and bang on the drum that he most always carry with him. David One-wound and Ernest Bitternose is bare to the waist and carry what could pass for lances but is really sticks with a little crepe paper what was left over from Easter tied around them. Bedelia have me get out my ten gallon hat and put on Eathen's chaps, and she borrow me some spurs and a coil of rope so's I can look like a real cowboy. Frank and Connie wrap blankets around themselves and knowing them, I'm afraid to check to see if they got anything on under. The rest of the group, there is about fifteen altogether go dressed like regular Indians. We all drive down in Louis Coyote's pickup truck. We turn into the paved driveway and go about a hundred yards up to a white wood gate. The gate got on it a sign in red and white lettering: Brotherhood of the Burning Bush Bible College, Private Property, Trespassers Will Be Prosecuted. This Means You!

"Friendly people," say Connie.

The building that say "administration" on it be new, low, wide, have a flat roof, but it still got at the front some stained glass say, "Bible College" in blue, with in front of it a red burning bush that I bet look really pretty when the setting sun shines on it.

Inside, the building smell somewhere between a government office and a church. The air be thick with varnish and plastic, while the place have venetian blinds with no dust on them and rubbery looking plants grow out of tin buckets full of white stones. There is a girl at the front desk have her hair pulled tight in a bun, so tight it make her eyes bulge a little. She have a face like a new red potato and her ears stick out like cup handles. I always wonder if places like this can only get ugly girls to work in them or if ugly girls go looking for places like this to work.

"We'd like to see Mr. Bush," says Frank, but Bedelia bat him hard in the ribs as he say it.

"How did you get in here?" the secretary says, and pushes real hard on a white button built into the edge of her desk. We can hear a buzzing off in the distance like a trapped wasp.

"We'd like to see the...manager," say Bedelia, being real polite.

"You know, the head honcho," says Frank, and gets his ribs poked again for his trouble.

"Dr. Manson never sees anyone without an appointment," say the secretary, and sniff up her little-pig-nose. Just then three guys come run into the room, two students who be pale and blond, wear sky-blue blazers and grey pants like all the students at the college, and a guy dressed like one of these here Commissionaires who are kind of play-policemen, usually retired army guys who enjoy pushing people around.

"What's going on here, Julie?" the guard guy say, pulling with his right hand at his belt like he wishes he had a gun there.

"These people..."

"We come to see the manager..."

"He's out," says the guard.

"We'll wait," we say, and start to make ourselves comfortable on the cherry-colored sofa and the two square lemon-colored chairs with chrome handles.

"You'll have to leave," says the guard, who got shiny black side burns and puffy red cheeks and nose.

"You gonna make us?" says Eathen Firstrider, moving up front to show he is about a half a foot taller than the guard, and have a hunting knife in his belt.

"Dr. Manson won't be back until next week," he say.

"That's okay, we'll wait," says Eathen.

"Boo!" says Connie Bigcharles as she take a couple of quick steps toward the two students who stand looking stupid as if they ain't been out in the sunlight for years. The students jump back then look silly at each other to realize they been scared by a girl in a blanket.

Just then a blond-wood door have 'Private' in black letters across it, open and out come a really large man look like a yellow-headed buzzard. He have to duck his head to come through the door, be all dressed in black except for a white collar like a ring of snow around his neck. He have a long red face look like it belong to a farmer been driving his tractor for a week, all this is topped with yellow hair the colour of ripe barley.

"Is there a problem?" he says.

"They broke in, Dr. Manson," says the guard.

"Why are you here?" he says to us, his voice is even and his eyes ain't scared like the others.

"We came to talk some business with you," says Bedelia.

"Are you from the reserve?" We nod.

"Then come in … you're always welcome here," he say and gesture toward his office with a hand look like it fixed a few tractors in its day.

His presence make us all kind of quiet. "We don't all have to come in if it be too crowded," says Bedelia.

"Quite all right," says Dr. Manson. "Julie, get coffee for our visitors, please."

"Sure you ain't got no beer?" says Frank, who ain't

been caught up in the mood yet. But he get the idea when
Bedelia elbow his ribs, I stomp his toes, and even Connie
punch at his arm some.

His office is big and light and look out on the rolling
lawn full of beds of yellow and maroon flowers. Me,
Bedelia and Eathen sit on chairs while the rest stand or
sit on the green carpet floor. Dr. Manson sit behind a
desk that is all chrome and clear plastic so he don't
appear to be hiding from us the way business and church
people usually do.

"Now suppose you tell me why you're here?" he says.

As Bedelia talk, Dr. Manson take out a black fountain
pen from inside his suit. The pen sort of get lost in his big
hand but he make notes on a pad of white paper and the
scratchy sound of the pen and Bedelia's voice be the only
sounds in the room for a long time.

"You've made some excellent points, Bedelia," Dr.
Manson say when she stop talking. He was introduced
to us only once but he remembers all our names. The
secretary has put a big glass coffee pot on his desk and
he say things like, "Would you like some more coffee,
Eathen?" and, "Help yourself to the sugar, Frank," after
he see Frank is busy chewing up sugar cubes. When he
says these things he always look at the right Indian. He
is not like most white men we have to deal with but it
easy to tell he is not the type to fool around with either.

"I've only been here a short time but I'm afraid we
here at the college are very isolated from the community.
Our job is to provide Christian education for young
people from all over North America and sometimes the
world. I've been advised by my board of directors that
the lease is coming up for renewal and that no problems
are anticipated. I agree with you that for using your land
we should make a significant contribution to your
community..."

It is here that Bedelia jump in to explain more about
how we got ten times more alcoholics and people with
drug problems than ordinary places, and how the suicide

rates be 25 times that of white people, and how there been over 20 violent deaths on the reserve in the last year, like people getting runned over by cars and getting beat or burned to death.

Dr. Manson shake his big yellow head. "I will make definite recommendations to my board of directors, but the college seems obligated to deal with Chief Crow-eye and the Tribal Council…"

"You leave that to us," says Bedelia, and the rest of us nod. "You be dealing with the Ermineskin Warrier Society soon enough." That sound good when we say it but as Mad Etta our medicine lady say, it is all talking down a gopher hole.

Dr. Manson then take us on a little tour of the college, show us their cafeteria that can feed 250 people at once, and the gym that be twice as big and ten times as new as Blue Quills Hall. Bedelia ask a lot of questions about money and Dr. Manson bring into our meeting a fellow called Brother Schram who I guess be kind of the book-keeper for the college 'cause he got thick blue-coloured books under his arm and he dig down into them with his nose close to the pages when Dr. Manson ask a question.

"Our total charitable budget was $127,000," Brother Schram says, "of which $57,000 was directed to our projects in Botswana, $40,000 to Pakistan, $25,000 to Bangladesh, and $5,000 miscellaneous donations."

"That's us," says Frank, "miscellaneous."

"I thought you could get shots for it now," says Connie.

"How much was spent here in Alberta?" says Dr. Manson.

"Well, let me see, yes, here it is. We gave $50 to the United Way Appeal in Wetaskiwin, and $5.00 goodwill advertising to the Ponoka High School newspaper."

Later, as we are leaving, Dr. Manson shake hands on all of us and wish us good luck.

"Do you think we been had?" I say to Bedelia as we walk back to the truck.

"I'm not sure."

"Guy like him could talk us into joining the cavalry," says Frank, and this time there ain't nobody to disagree with him.

What we told Dr. Manson we might do is a lot easier to talk about than accomplish. Nobody's ever tried to cross Chief Tom and Samantha, especially at one of their meetings. Hardly nobody ever go to these here Tribal Council meetings. I went once and there was just Chief Tom, Samantha, about four or five people who follow them around like hungry dogs and do whatever they is told, and a half dozen old people who was early for the bingo game. Samantha is the one who really run things. She have lots of notes on her clipboard and always tell Chief Tom what they should do next. That night Chief Tom read off a whole page of stuff that be all full of Government words like whereas and the party of the first part, but by listening real close it seem to me that it be arranging to give Chief Tom and Samantha, as Chief and Secretary, a whole lot more money for keeping on to do not much of anything.

When he finish Chief Tom look all around with his beady little eyes like a sparrow, then he say, "Will somebody make that a motion?" One of his friends raise up a hand. "Seconder?" say Chief Tom, and another friend put up his hand. "Discussion," say the Chief, then add right after it, "All in favour." The friends and the bingo players raise up their hands. "Carried," say Chief Tom, while I'm still sit there think about the discussion part.

Bedelia and me do some more digging, this time in some old boxes of files in the office at Blue Quills Hall and we find that any Indian over 18 can vote at a Tribal Council Meeting.

A couple of weeks later me and Bedelia go back to see Dr. Manson. I guess he left instructions 'cause neither the guard or the secretary give us any trouble and the secretary bring coffee without being asked.

"I had a meeting with your Chief," Dr. Manson say,

"and it appears that there are a number of problems, the main one being that Chief Crow-eye doesn't recognize the existence of your organization—The Ermineskin Warrier Society. He thinks you are a group of children, in fact, 'Boys will be boys,' is the way he described you," he say looking right at Bedelia, who clench her teeth together. "Chief Crow-eye is quite happy, in fact he insists on renewing the lease exactly as is."

"At her home Bedelia's got a pet rock that she named Chief Tom," I say. We all have us a little laugh about that.

"I honestly don't know what I can do to help you," Dr. Manson say. "I'll try to get the directors of the college to interest themselves in the plight of your people..."

"Just let us know when the lease renewal coming up at the Tribal Council," say Bedelia.

One idea we have was that maybe we could get a Cree Indian student into the BBBBC. We figure somewhere there must be an Indian would want to be a minister. Then if a Cree graduate they could get lots of that church money to use of good things on the reserve.

"If you didn't live in Canada, it would be all right," say Dr. Manson. "We could give a scholarship if you were from the Third World, China or even Mexico, but as a Canadian you'd have to pay full tuition."

We all groan.

"Sometimes it is very difficult to retain one's serenity in circumstances such as these," he say, and smile by crinkling up the skin around his grey eyes. He pick up the rock paperweight on his desk like he going to crush it in his big, rough hand.

The day of the Tribal Council Meeting we got about 25 people, including my mother, my brother Joseph who don't think so good, and Blind Louis Coyote, rounded up in case we need them. We waiting for Dr. Manson and Brother Schram as they come walk up from the parking lot to Blue Quills Hall.

"What about the things we talked about?" Bedelia say to Dr. Manson. We kept in touch with him and we know that he been off the last couple of days at one of them Board of Directors meetings in Calgary.

"I'm afraid not, my dear. I explained your situation to the Board of Directors, I tried to be persuasive, but they are committed to our policy of furthering international relations," and he smile sad at us and put a kind hand on Bedelia's shoulder.

At the meeting we only bring in about six people but we got the rest ready when we need them. Chief Tom and Samantha read up and down her clipboard a few times, I guess trying to figure what us guys could be interested in.

"Well, what are you doing here, young people?" Chief Tom say and smile like somebody put a finger on each side of his mouth and pushed, while his eyes go all around the hall about three times.

"Who, us?" we say. "We just waiting to play volleyball later on. You having a meeting or something?"

"Nothing that would interest you," say the Chief. "Just a business meeting." But there is a long wait while one of Chief Tom's friends, Joe Wolfchild, go out and come back with more people so that they got us outnumbered.

The Chief read off a couple of items that him and his friends approve quick while we try not to act interested.

"The Bible College lease is up for renewal. We recommend that it be renewed for another fifty years at a dollar a year. Somebody make that a motion?" Frank Fence-post gone back and opened the door and the basketball stands fill up with 20 or so of our people. Up go Joe Wolfchild's hand. "Seconder," say Chief Tom, and Elsie Wolfchild wave her hand in the air.

"Discussion." And nobody make a sound.

"All in favour?" And up go the ten or so hands he brought in.

"Carried," say the Chief.

"Whoa!" says Bedelia Coyote, "don't you have to asked who's opposed?"

"Oh, yes," say the Chief and he look kind of uneasy. "Opposed?" and all our people put up a hand. Frank Fence-post and my brother Joseph I think put up both of theirs.

"They're not qualified to vote," say Samantha in a harsh voice and wave her slim brown arm in our direction.

"We're all over 18 and we're all Crees," I hear myself saying. "We got as much right to vote as anybody." Our people cheer. Chief Tom and Samantha having a little conference and the Chief's eyes seem to flash red even through his new glasses. Not long ago Samantha got him a pair of blue tinted glasses. Since then Frank has taken to calling him Old Blue Eyes, and once when Chief Tom walked into the Gold Nugget Cafe in Wetaskiwin Frank said, "Hey, you figure you can pass for white with those glasses," and got himself a look that could stop a charging buffalo right in his tracks.

Bedelia is up on her feet now and is making a motion that go on for a long time—she name how much rent got to be paid—how to keep the land they got to provide breakfast in their cafeteria for all the Hobbema school kids, and how they got to hire councillors to start programmes…everybody is jump up and down some and I bet when she finish we is all gonna second that motion together.

I look over at Dr. Manson and he be nodding his head as Bedelia talk.

For now, every one of us is happy. We winning the battle, but I bet the war gonna go on for a long time.

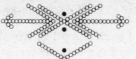

NESTS

"CLOSE THE GODDAMN door, Silas," Mr. Moon says to me.

"The door is closed," I answer him. Mr. Gus Moon is sitting at his kitchen table with his back to the door. The cook-stove is fired up until the stove lids look dull red, the colour of some of the leaves that are blowing around the yard.

"Made a hell of a draft when you came in. I'm freezing all the time," and he shake his hunched-up shoulders and take a big drink from a heavy white coffee mug. He is wearing a black sweater that somebody knit for him, the wool is thick and look like little links of logging chain. Under that he got on a plaid work-shirt, buttoned right up to the neck, bib-overalls, and I'm pretty sure that underneath is some of that Stanfield's underwear, the thick kind, the colour of barley and just about as scratchy.

"Have some coffee, Silas. It'll warm you up."

"It's pretty warm out today, Mr. Moon. See how nice the sun's shining." In that kitchen it must be a hundred above, or more. I start to sweat as soon as I step inside. "Tell me what you'd like done today and I'll get started," I say. This is, I guess, the third weekend I been working on Mr. Moon's farm. He is a white farmer, live down toward Ponoka. I seen his ad in the *Wetaskiwin Times,* want somebody to help out on weekends. His house is big, and old; it ain't painted but he got inside-plumbing and electricity, though he heats the place with a big wood stove. Mr. Moon been sick for a while and not able to do his own work.

"Have some coffee, Silas," Gus Moon say to me in a voice that don't leave me no choice.

"Where do you want your mail?" I say. I'm holding two newspapers I pulled out of the metal mailbox down by the road.

"Just put them there on the sideboard."

I pour some coffee from the blue-enamel pot that stands on the back of the stove and sit down. There is a can of Carnation milk on the table, got a triangular hole punched on each side of the lid, but the sugar bowl is empty. My coffee is boiled and bitter; I like it with lots of sugar. I unzip my jacket, take it off and hang it on the back of my chair. I'm too hot even in just a tee-shirt and jeans, but Mr. Moon sit hunched over the table the way cold people do. Mr. Moon used to have a wife, named Jessie, I know because he talks about her once in a while. But I can't figure out whether she's dead, run off, or just away somewhere. Only other person live with him is his daughter, Danielle, who is about fifteen.

Danielle is the kind of white girl I have dreams about just before I go to sleep at night. She have dark blue eyes in a tanned face, long black hair that come down below her shoulders when it straight, but sometimes she curl it and twist it and pile it up on top of her head. Her teeth are shiny white. She is slim and have nice breasts, look like apples under the yellow sweater she usually wears.

That remind me of the funniest thing about this here farm, they grow apples. You can grow apples in this country but they is hard and bitter and not much good for anything but feed hogs or make home brew. But down about a hundred yards in front of the kitchen window is a patch of apple trees, must be over a hundred of them, the leaves mainly gone this time of year. Them trees is scrunched up as crippled men, some of their trunks twisted like a chicken neck that been wrung.

"They was *her* idea, them trees," Gus Moon said to me the first day I was here, after he seen me staring out the window at them. "Bringing *them* in here was her idea too," he say, and point to where there is two wasp nests each hanging by a thread from the ceiling, twirl first one way then another. They is dark as clouds hanging there in the room full of bright fall sunlight. Gus Moon hardly let me get any work done that day. In fact, I have hardly done any work at all. Mainly I just sit in the kitchen and listen to him talk. He cusses out the wasp nests and wasps in general and the apple trees, and worries out loud about what Danielle is doing that she shouldn't. He sure does hate them wasps. Parasites is what he calls them. "Go down to the orchard and see what they do," he says to me in a loud voice. And later that first afternoon I do. All around was apples rotting on the ground. I could hear wasps buzzing but mainly couldn't see any. Then I noticed that those apples each got a hole in them, one hole like it been made with a bullet. I picked one up and it was light as paper, been hollowed out by them wasps. Another one I pick up be almost alive—I could hear them buzz and feel the vibration, a thrill like holding my hand close to a power saw.

That first day I come to work here, Mr. Moon sitting just like he is now; he was watching somebody moving around down among the apple trees. I didn't know it was Danielle until she come into the house a few minutes later. He introduce me to her, but she look at me like all she seen was the chair I'm sitting on.

"I've been watching you," Mr. Moon says, "You know that?"

"I know," Danielle says in a real snotty voice. "I see you there. *We* see you there."

"Then why don't you stay to hell out of that orchard, like I've told you?"

"I wasn't doing anything," she says, this time in kind of a dreamy voice. Then, "Did the newspapers come?"

Mr. Moon got his head slumped over his coffee almost like he was praying.

"They're on the sideboard there," Mr. Moon says. Danielle start across the kitchen.

"Don't you go cutting them up until I've had a chance to look at them," Mr. Moon says.

"You never look at them," says Danielle as she picks up the papers and begins pushing stuff around on the sideboard.

"What are you lookin' for, girl?"

"The scissors. Here they are." She picked up a big pair of silver scissors and started right in cutting them newspapers, not like she was cutting out pictures but big stabbing cuts in all directions.

"I told you not to do that," Mr. Moon yell. "All you do is make scraps." I sure wish I was someplace else.

"They're not scraps," Danielle says real calmly. "They're clippings. I like clippings, they make my room nicer."

"It ain't your room you put 'em in. Ain't your room you do all that cutting and pasting for. And look at the sideboard and the table and the floor...whole place stinks of glue."

"It's a nice smell. Clean..."

Mr. Moon is right about the smell. The whole room is filled with the odour of glue. And I notice now that the sideboard have bits of paper stuck to it, and the table have gluey patches.

"The whole place stinks. And don't tell me about cuttin'. Why look at that piece in your hand you cut that fellow's..."

"Don't upset yourself, Father. I know what I'm doing. *I* cut and paste things and *you* stare out the window..."

"At least I know why I'm here."

"Sometimes I think you do," Danielle says. I sure don't know what they're talking about. Danielle gathers up the papers and scissors and a big bottle of glue and starts toward the stairs when all of a sudden she drops the glue. The top comes off and it spills on the floor.

"Now look what you done. Get a cloth."

Danielle gets a dirty cloth from beside the old black and silver stove, but instead of wiping up the glue she spreads it out in a sticky circle.

"Hey, stop that. You're makin' a bigger mess."

"Am I?" she says, and stares up at him with a real strange look in her eyes. Then she stands up and walks back and forth in the sticky patch she's made.

"Stop dancin' in that muck," her father yells.

They fight some more and she finally goes upstairs. After that Mr. Moon puts some more wood in the stove, cook himself up more coffee, and about the only work I get to do is to wash up the sticky mess from the floor.

The next week when I get there, the kitchen is as hot as ever, Mr. Moon is in his same place and I swear the argument has taken up where it left off.

"Why haven't you been at school?" Mr. Moon yell at Danielle.

"I have. You know I'm a very good student, Father."

"You lie. The principal phoned and said you haven't been but about one day a week since the term started."

"He must be mistaken, Father. You know how schools get their records mixed up."

"And you shouldn't oughta take that dress Martin and Maggie bought ya. I heard you lying to them on the phone about how well you was doing in school."

"They bought it for me because they like me. It's yellow, they know that's my favorite colour. Uncle Martin says I'm pretty. Do you think I'm pretty, Father?"

"Sure you're pretty. You're just like your mama."

There is a long silence after he says that, as if they've both agreed not to talk about the mother. They live too far from the reserve for any other Indians to know them and I don't know any white folks way down here, well enough to ask about the Moons.

"Mama was beautiful, wasn't she?" says Danielle, and she walks across to where there is a small mirror on the wall. She taken some yellow ribbons and weaved them in and out of her hair what is piled up on top of her head today. "Do you like my hair like this, Father?" she say. He don't answer right away. I sure do think she's pretty. I don't know whether to tell her so or not. I would, but I can see her eyes in the mirror and there is something not right; her eyes is bright and clear, but they are too bright, almost as if they are a few degrees out of focus.

Gus don't ever answer the question. He get distracted by how cold he is and for the rest of the afternoon he have me nail weather-stripping around the door both inside and out, and around the big bay window that look out on the apple orchard.

It don't look like this week is gonna be any different. The room is boiling. Mr. Moon is cold. And he is still mad at everybody, especially Danielle. I don't figure I'm gonna come here any more. I'd rather do hard work than sit around listen to white people argue. But I hardly get started on my coffee when a truck pull up in the yard, and Mr. Moon's brother Martin come into the house.

I can tell they is brothers. Gus Moon look older, though I don't know whether he is or not. Both of them got short hair, windburned skin, and each of them got big ears stick out from their heads.

"You cold, Marty?" is the first words Gus say after he introduce me.

"The only reason you feel cold is because you keep it so warm in here."

Mr. Gus Moon just point out the window. "Marty, you see them few leaves flutterin' on the branches? I tell you, when the wind's strong enough to move them stocky little trees around why it's cold out there. Wind seems to blow right through the house these days," his voice trail off and he shiver.

"Come on, Gus, You got to make some effort. You want to play cards? Or maybe we could go into town later; there's some Golden Glove Boxing at the Legion Hall tonight."

"No. Thanks, Marty, I don't feel good enough to go out."

"Well, pour me some coffee then."

"You can't have it the way you like it. There's no sugar. The kid eats it all up. Got a powerful cravin' for sweets, just like her mother."

"You worry too much about Danielle," says Martin. "She seems fine to us. It's only natural for you to worry after what happened, but Danielle's fine—she's a real little princess."

"You don't have any idea what's goin' on, do ya, Marty?"

"Let's stop beating around the bush, Gus. What's wrong with you? I talked with Doc Fowler in Ponoka and he says there's no reason you can't go back to work. You should be outside getting exercise."

"It's too cold."

"What the hell are you talking about, Gus? Why are you afraid of the weather? Hell, we got Indian summer coming up yet." After he say that he look over at me and his eyes get big. "No offence," he say.

"No offence," I answer.

"Winter ain't far off," says Gus in his tired voice. "Plenty of work needs doin'."

"The place *is* starting to look rundown," says Martin. "Why don't you put this kid to work outside instead of keeping him sitting in here?"

"I was gonna have him cut down them apple trees, stack them and burn them. But don't expect it makes much difference now."

"I can think of a lot of things that need doing worse.

Them trees were Jessie's, and Danielle loves them. Why don't you let me come over and help out for a few days. Maggie and I would both come over. Danielle needs a woman to talk to…"

"No she don't."

"We just want to help."

"I can do for myself. For us. I just need to get the tractor fixed."

"What's wrong with it?" says Martin.

"Parts missin'. Indians I figure. Them buggers will steal you blind if you give them half a chance." Then he looks at me. "Sorry Silas, I didn't mean you."

"You got some work for me to do, Mr. Moon?" I ask.

"Yeah, in a while. Have some more coffee."

Then Mr. Moon stare hard out the window. "Look, way down at the far end of the orchard. There's somebody there, I know it."

"What if there is?" says Martin, squinting up his eyes. "It would only be Danielle."

I look out the window too, and I think I spot something yellow moving way at the end of the orchard.

"Only," yell Mr. Moon. "I've told her never to go down there. Never to hang around them…"

"Come on, Gus. It's nothing to get excited about. Let's play cards."

"Ain't got no cards."

"You always got a couple of decks on the sideboard there," says Martin and starts across the room.

"Danielle took 'em."

"Danielle doesn't play cards. Maggie and me couldn't even get her to learn rummy."

"She takes 'em up to that room."

"What are you talking about, Gus?" Martin Moon even looks over at me in case I know what's going on, but I just shrug my shoulders.

Martin stops and examines the wasp's nests; he watches them twirl slow in the heat of the room. "Why have you still got these things around, Gus? These, you should get rid of."

"Danielle about throws a fit every time I mention it. God, but it's cold, Marty," and I think I can hear Mr. Moon's teeth chattering. "Ever had a close look at one of them things, Marty?"

Martin got a big, sausage-fingered hand on each side of one of the nests.

"They sure are a work of art, ain't they?" Martin says.

"You know what they do, Marty? Wasps kidnap bugs and ants and spiders, stuff them into those little sections to use for food later on."

"Yeah? Look at all the compartments in this thing, and it feels like real paper, like cardboard. I wonder how…?"

"Goddamn wasps," yell Gus Moon. "It was them caused all the trouble. There are other nests down in the orchard. If she hasn't moved them already."

"Easy, Gus. Jessie wasn't well, we all know that. You can't go blaming yourself. You got to think about going back to work."

"I ain't never going back to work. Don't you understand? First Jessie and now Danielle."

"Danielle? There's nothing wrong with Danielle. And you got to stop blaming yourself for what happened to Jessie."

"I should have done something or told somebody, way back when she started fixing up that spare room…for whatever it was she was…expecting."

"For Danny?" asks Martin.

"No. No. She started turning that spare bedroom into a…a nursery maybe. She papered the walls, and then papered them again, and again. Cats, ducks, lambs, elephants, one layer on top of the other. And furniture; jammed in until things had to be piled on top of one another. And curtains; cut the room up like it was a checker board, cords running every which-way each one holding up curtain material. And never a word of explanation. She just stared at me with that far-off look in her eyes, just stared at me like she was doing me a favour."

Gus Moon stops talking and lets out a long sigh, like he's glad he's finally told somebody about what is bothering him. His brother just sits, looking a little like he's been punched real hard. Martin takes his coffee cup, lifts it half-way to his mouth, then sets it down on the table with a clunk; the reason he set it down was because his hand was shaking so hard.

"You sure, Gus?" Martin finally says in a small voice.

"Goddammit, Marty, you don't believe me do ya?" shouts Gus.

"I don't..."

"You want to see it, Marty? Top of the stairs, first door on the left. That is if Danielle will let you in. She practically lives in there. Bassinettes and curtains and cardboard and junk, and yellow dresses. You want to see in there, Marty?"

"I know it must be right, if you say it is." says Martin. If a person's voice can be pale, his sure is. By accident, I know that what Gus Moon says is true. First time I asked to use the bathroom, Mr. Gus just pointed to the upstairs. Looking for the bathroom I opened the door he is talking about now, and it was just the way he describe it, all full of cloth and furniture and smelling of glue. And I think just from the quick look I had that some of them rows of cloth been joined together with glue and paper so the room is divided up in little sections just like a bee's nest.

"You're damn right I'm right, Marty. It started with Jessie wantin' another baby. I mean, I thought she'd get over it. Other women do." He stop for a minute, take a drink from his coffee cup, shiver and go on. "You aren't cold, are you, Marty? How about you, Silas?" We both shake our heads. "You know, sometimes I stand here at this window, and I see her down there among the apple trees. See her plain as day. There was more to it than her just being crazy. The things she used to do…" While he is talking I see a little motion in the corner of the room and Danielle comes in from the back of the house. She is wearing a yellow dress. It look like the kind I've seen at high school graduations in Wetaskiwin, lots and lots of layers of stiff, lacy-like material. She look really beautiful, but kind of scary too. She stands listening to her papa and I sure don't like the look on her face or in her eyes.

"You know, towards the end she'd stay down there all day long. Spend all the daylight hours just watching them do whatever those, those bastards do." Martin catches sight of Danielle and motions for Gus to stop talking but Gus don't pay no attention until Martin breaks in on him.

"Well, here's Danny, and don't she look pretty in that dress. Your aunty will sure be proud of how you look."

Danielle doesn't seem to hear him. Her eyes look at and through her father. She speaks slow and careful but I can tell she is so mad she holding her hands together to keep them from shaking.

"Why don't you tell Uncle Martin how you hated them, Father? Tell him how you tried to make them go away, how you sneaked down to the orchard in the night with a torch and tried to destroy them. Tell him how Mother threw herself on you and saved them."

"Danny, what is this?" says Martin.

"Am I right, Father? Didn't you always hate them, call them…"

"Parasites," yell Gus Moon in a loud voice. He stands up from the table tip over his coffee.

"That's right, Father. Parasites. 'Predacious bastards,' isn't that what you always said?"

"Yes. Bastards! Parasites!" yells Gus Moon. "Marty, you believe me now, don't you? She'd go right up to them. Right up close. Right to the nest; she'd stand there and rub her cheek on it. She'd hum and sway and they'd, they'd…"

"They'd swarm her," says Danielle, crossing the kitchen and staring across the table and out toward the rows and rows of twisted trees. Her father is standing too, glaring at her, his cheeks and chin covered in gray stubble; his eyes hid deep in his face look glazed like a sick animal. "It was a ritual. She was the host. You couldn't stop it. You did all that was required of you, Father. You shouldn't feel bad about anything. You've served your purpose…"

"What the hell are you talking about, Danielle?" says Martin.

"She believes all the stuff that her mother told her. It's all crap. Jessie was crazy. She'd stand there swayin', them yellow things crawling across her skin. She took off her clothes…"

"They never hurt her," says Danielle. "There was never a mark."

Mr. Gus Moon's shoulders are slumped even more as he stares at his daughter. "Sometimes when I think I see Jessie down there in the orchard, I expect it's Danielle I'm seein', though I don't want it to be."

"We see you watching from the window," says Danielle, her voice excited, like she just won an argument.

Martin just sits shaking his head; his lips form words he wants to say to Danielle, but no sound comes out of his mouth.

"Who can survive it, Marty?" Gus Moon says in kind of a croak.

"They survive, Father," says Danielle.

"First snow, Marty," says Gus, "I'm a dead man."

VOWS

REASON I GET involved in the trouble is that Ray Smith take courses with me at the Technical School in Wetaskiwin. He is learn to be a sheet metal worker and be a pretty good dude. Biggest problem he have until the business with Julie Dodginghorse be his own family.

The Smiths is kind of a wild bunch. Old October Smith have about four wives at different times and each one have a lot of kids, some that are October's and some not. Ray got sisters named Peaches, Pears and Plums. They say they was named for whatever was on the kitchen cupboard on the day they was born. Smiths live in a log cabin with a sod roof and walls chinked with moss and cow shit. Some of the older boys is bad dudes and one of them committed a murder here a few years ago. Some of the girls gone to the city and disappeared the way our Indian girls do.

"You know what happened to me?" Ray say to me one morning while we waiting for our English class to start. "This morning when I come out of my cabin Julie's old man is sit in that shiny red pickup of Hofstetter's that he drives.

"'Get in, Ray.' he says to me, 'I'll drive you to school.'

"What he tell me while we driving is that he got plans for Julie—university and all that—and he don't want her getting tied up at 16 with a guy like me. Not that I'm so bad, he says. I try to be polite with him. I tell him how much Julie and me care for each other and how even though I'd like for everyone to be happy we're gonna keep on seeing each other.

"Well, when he hear that he just puff out his big chest like a partridge.

"'Ray,' he says to me. 'you keep away from Julie from now on or I'll see that you get kicked out of the Tech School.'

"You think he can do that, Silas?"

"He's buddies with Chief Tom. Being an MLA and an Indian Chief let Chief Tom do about anything he wants to."

"He said too that some of my brothers and sisters got white blood in them and he could make trouble for them too 'cause Métis ain't allowed to live on the reserve. Then he end up by saying to me, 'You ever thought about who your father might have been?'"

"Look like he hold all the cards," I say. "What you plan on doing?" I'm trying to think what I would do if my girl's father told me something like that.

"All I know is we ain't gonna stop going together," says Ray, a real troubled look on his face.

Ray is 19 years old, average tall, thin, and his shoulders stoop over a bit. He wear gold-rimmed glasses and when he have money get his hair cut at a barber shop in Wetaskiwin and puffed out on the sides to cover up his ears. He don't get mean when he drink and never been sent to jail.

Most families wouldn't mind if he went after one of their daughters. But then Melvin Dodginghorse don't figure that his is "most" families.

Ray and Julie first took to one another a couple of months ago at a Saturday night dance at Blue Quills

Hall here on the reserve. It easy to see why Ray like her. Julie is tiny, not even five feet high, I bet. She got hair that comes all the way down touch the belt of her jeans at the back. And she have so much energy she bounce wherever she going and she have a laugh like a happy bird you hear early in the morning.

She don't often come to the dances and probably wasn't supposed to be there. Her parents is snooty. They is red on the outside but if you was to cut them they'd bleed white blood.

Melvin Dodginghorse used to be a champion cowboy and he married a Blood lady who worked in a Government office in Lethbridge. A lady who wear dresses all year round and own a fur coat been bought in a store in Edmonton. They live in an Indian Affairs built house what they fenced and painted white. Melvin built onto the house a two car garage and they got a lawn with flower beds. Melvin work as a foreman for Hofstetter Cattle Co. in Wetaskiwin and he is a close friend of Chief Tom Crow-eye and his girlfriend, Samantha Yellow-knees. People say Melvin paid a hundred dollars to help Chief Tom get elected MLA for Wetaskiwin in the Conservative Government.

What people like them would want for their daughter is to go to university and then marry a white man. My sister marry a white man, all on her own, and I guess she is happy, but it make the rest of us sad.

Julie's folks made it almost impossible for her and Ray to be together. But not quite. She still claim she going to a girlfriend's to study or she skip her dance lesson in Wetaskiwin so they can walk in the park together.

"You know what's the really funny thing?" say Ray, rolling his cue back and forth on the dirty green cloth of the table at the Hobbema Pool Hall. "We wasn't planning on get married for a long time. Not until Julie finish school and I got me a good job. But if we can't see each other at all then we have to make a move of some kind."

Some of us we think about Mad Etta our Medicine Lady.

"What if Etta was to marry you?" we say.

"What good would that do? Only old time Indians believe in Etta. We dealing with white people here," say Ray.

"Yeah," I add. "Government don't recognize Indian ceremonies. To be legal you got to be married by someone who got a Government license."

We all go home feeling helpless. But word get around the way rumours do that Ray and Julie either are going to, or have already been married by Mad Etta.

Next evening Melvin Dodginghorse screech his truck to a stop outside Mad Etta's cabin and he step out of it so quick he get swallowed up in the dust he made by stopping. He give one knock at the door and then open it without waiting.

Mad Etta look at him with a steady stare with her eyes that be deep down in her face.

"Listen, Old Woman," Melvin Dodginghorse say, "I love my daughter and I'm gonna do the best for her. Don't you marry my daughter and that..."

"What you gonna do to me if I do?" says Etta, tipping back her bottle of Lethbridge Pale Ale. Etta is sitting on her tree-trunk chair, with the light behind her so she look big as a bear. "Chief Tom checked with his lawyer and he says as long as Julie's under age it don't matter who does the ceremony, it ain't valid."

"If it wouldn't be no good, why are you here yelling at me?"

"Because I don't want the bother of it. I know how to look after my daughter and by God, I fix Ray Smith good..."

"If I marry them you gonna take away my license to marry people? My powers come down through the generations. Chief Tom's all come from pieces of Government white paper. His power can be voted away from him. You can't do that to me."

"Old Woman, you ain't got no powers." And it real funny to me to hear Melvin Dodginghorse switch from English to Cree when he get madder. "You stick to making up medicine bags to cure aching joints. I live in the real world and I don't believe in you and I'm telling you to stay out of my life or you be sorry..." and he turn around and slam out of the door.

"Make him feel better to yell at somebody," says Etta, looking buffalo big in her corner. "It tough to decide who right, if anybody is. We don't learn nothing in thousands of years...parents still want to run the lives of their kids. It was more simple when I was young. You know how I got a husband?"

I know Etta is gonna tell me anyway.

"Bunch of us girls was out berrying. Lawrence, he rode his pony along behind me. That was all it took. I ran home and told my father. He said he guessed Lawrence was all right except that he was so small, and we went and set up a teepee near where Lawrence's family was camped. I went and took Lawrence a pair of moccasins I made myself with lots of bright quills on them. When he accept the moccasins from me that meant he take me as his wife, and him and me moved into the teepee my folks had put up. Bet my father was just as happy not to have to hunt to feed me no more," Etta says laughing and patting her five-flour-sack dress.

I remember that afternoon Julie Dodginghorse saying "'What do you see in him? What do you see in him?' My old man keeps asking me, and I can't tell him anything. How can you tell another person what love feels like?"

I tell this to Mad Etta.

"You hear people say that all the time. It is just as much a mystery as why the birds know to fly away in the fall or a rabbit knows to grow white fur for the winter.

"You never know my man, did you, Silas? He die about the year you was born. People always say that about us. 'What's he see in her?' I never know. Lawrence was small and skinny as your friend Rufus Firstrider, and I'm fat and mean as six minks in a cage. If I'd ever rolled over on him in the night would of killed him for sure." Etta take a drink from her beer. "But Lawrence have a good heart. He always treat me best as he was able and I done the same for him."

Next morning Ray meet me in the hall at the Tech School with kind of a blank look on his face.

"They kicked me out, Silas," he say to me, and wave a sheet of paper signed by the school principal. We go and talk to my friend Mr. Nichols but he say there probably ain't much he can do though he'll look into it.

Next morning Melvin Dodginghorse's truck have all its tires cut and somebody throwed mud all over their white painted house. The balls of mud slid down the white siding leaving marks like black tears.

It is Ray's little brothers, who been raised up wild as coyotes, and their friends who done it. "I told them not to," Ray say over and over. "It only make things worse."

"My papa blames Ray for doing it all by himself," Julie says to us when she run from her mother's car into the General Store the next afternoon. "He says it just shows what kind of a bad person Ray is."

"The sad thing is," says Ray, "is that Mr. Dodginghorse and me we got almost the same ideas. It ain't like I was a bush Indian gonna expect my wife to walk a trapline. I want for Julie and me a house like she lives in and I was gonna go out and work to get it. Only big difference between me and Melvin Dodginghorse is about 25 years of age."

Julie's parents keep her mostly a prisoner after that. To see her at all Ray has to sneak up to the school at lunch hour. Mrs. Dodginghorse drive her to and from school and one of them go everywhere with her on week-

ends and they always go to Wetaskiwin or Edmonton
and never do no Indian things here on the reserve.

"If Julie was just a couple of years older. I just don't
know what we can do," says Ray.

"You either got to act or give up," says Mad Etta.
"Nothing stand still for very long. It either go forward or
backward."

And it look like Ray gived up. Next Saturday night he
sit on the bench along the wall at Blue Quills. Most of the
girls come and dance with him at one time or another
but nobody can cheer him up.

"Why don't we go up and bust Julie out of her house?"
says my friend Frank Fence-post. Most of us have had a
few beers and it sound like a pretty good idea.

Funny how you can look at a place and never really
see it. Never noticed that in the new houses the bedroom
windows be small and high up on the side of the house.
And we got to guess which room is Julie's.

On the way we stop at Frank's cabin and pick up a
glass-cutter that he pick up as a five-finger-bargain from
McLeod's Store in Wetaskiwin because he liked how
shiny it was.

"We could just tap on the window," I suggest.

"How'd you like to have Melvin Dodginghorse staring
up your nose," says Frank. "We cut the window quiet-like
then lift up the curtains and see who's in there."

We have a hard time to reach the window at all. And
Dodginghorses don't have no junk in their yard that we
could pile under the window to stand on. We have to go in
the garage and wrestle out a 20 gallon oil drum. There is
six of us there, me, Frank, Connie Bigcharles, Eathen
and Rufus Firstrider, and Eathen's girl Julie Scar. It
pretty hard for that many people to be quiet. We hold
Frank's ankles as he stand on the barrel and the glass
cutter make squeaking noises like dragging a rubber
boot along hardwood.

"Oh, damn!" says Frank. And then, "Owww!" And

there is the sound of glass breaking on the floor inside.

"What the hell…" roar Melvin Dodginghorse's voice.

Frank pull up the curtains and say, "Trick or treat," drop them real quick again. Guess he didn't have much time to think of anything more clever to say.

We all run for Louis Coyote's pickup truck which we park down a hill and out of sight. On the way Frank get hung up on the metal gate and leave one half of his jean jacket flapping on the fence like washing.

"It was the side had the pocket with my wildwood flower in," he complain on the way back to the dance. Connie bandage up his hand with the other side of his jean jacket. We don't tell Ray what we tried, figure it only make him sadder.

On Monday, I walk with him up to the school at noon hour to see Julie.

"They going to send me to school in Edmonton," is the first thing she say to us. Then she tell how both her folks drove her up there on Sunday afternoon.

"It's a private Convent School, just like a prison. High windows and ceilings and the whole place smell of wax and incense. And the nuns glide around like their feet never touch the floor. And you got to wear *uniforms*. And you can't go out at night. And I can only come home once each term for a weekend."

"Leave us alone for a while, Silas," Ray say to me. And I do.

"Can you borrow the truck and drive us someplace tonight?" he say as we walk back toward our cabins.

"You and Julie gonna split tonight?"

"It ain't what we want to do. But it's what we got to do," says Ray.

That night Ray and I wait in the truck about a quarter mile from Dodginghorses and at about two in the morning Julie come to us. She jump into the truck and hug Ray's neck. The closing of the door sound to me like a gun shot and I jump some.

"They can't watch me all night," she say. "I just walk right out the front door."

I drive them where they tell me. Which is to a hill maybe ten miles in the bush.

Ray and Julie unload from the truck sleeping bags and backpacks. We borrowed stuff from everybody we know so they have lots of food, and one of them nylon tents that fold up to be about a foot square.

Behind them the sky is the deep blue of lake water. The moon and the Northern Lights turn everything strange colours. The birch trees are bare and white as chain lightning against the sky.

"Let Julie's folks think we gone to Edmonton or Calgary. If they have the police there looking for us it keep their minds busy. We're gonna make ourselves married, in our eyes. And it isn't anybody else that counts."

I shake their hands, wish them luck and walk to the truck.

When I look back they've turned and are facing each other the way I've seen couples do in church. I'm too far away to hear what they saying and I'm glad I am. It is better just to see their shapes dark against the bright night sky.

I release the brake on the truck and let it roll silent down the hill into the valley.

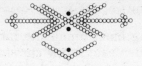

THE QUEEN'S HAT

WE SURE KNOW there going to be nothing but trouble when carloads of Government people come pussyfooting around the reserve. Groups of visiting white people usually have one leader who act like a mother duck, walk in front of the rest of the group and point out whatever it is they come to see: sometimes it is the school, or Blue Quills Hall, the hockey arena, or maybe they just come to stare at some of us real live Indians.

It depend on what kind of mood us Indians is in, on how we accept these groups. Sometimes we tear up the culvert in the road when we see the dust from their cars in the distance, make them walk up to the cabins, or sometimes we charge them money for us to put the culvert back. Other times we get them lost in the back country, or separate them from their cars, which they not likely to see in one piece again.

Back in September there was a group come around on a day when we all feeling like some company. We know we going to have some fun when we see Constable Chretien of the RCMP get out of the lead car. He is all decked up in his scarlet uniform. That mean there real important people with him. Behind Constable Chretien's police car is a long, black limousine, have a gold crest on the door, and when that fancy car stop, suit after suit climb out of it, stare around kind of wide-eyed, as if they ain't been away from tall buildings for a few years. Every one of them suits is stuffed with a white man.

One of them guys straightened his lapels, his glasses, and his back, walk toward me and my friends, speak to us in our language, Cree. We can understand him, but he speak Cree with what we call an Ottawa accent. He's learned his Cree from a book; he speak real formal, use full words and no slang.

"A very important person is going to visit this reserve next month," he say to us.

My friends are all gathered in a knot behind me. We have decided without anybody ever saying, that today we will behave like strangers on our own reserve. Before I can say anything, my friend Frank Fence-post push forward, stand himself at attention in front of the visitor.

"I am Fence-post, warrior, scout, medicine-person, spiritual advisor, champion rodeo performer, and I wash your car for only three dollars," Frank say in English. "I will be your interpreter, strange person."

"But *I* am an interpreter," say the man, after a long pause. He is dressed in an owl-grey suit, fit him tight as if it been painted on. "I am speaking to you in Cree, your native language," he say in Cree, but there is a funny tone to his voice, as if he is worried.

"Cree?" says Frank. "What is this Cree? Cree lives hundreds of miles north of here," and Frank wave his hand towards the west.

"Are you sure?" the man says in English. Then, "Do any of you understand me?" he yell in Cree. Everybody stay silent.

"Luckily Fence-post has travelled widely," says Frank. "Fence-post has been in jail in three provinces and two states. *I* will translate for *you*."

Frank turn to the ten or so of us that is standing

behind him, wave his arms in the air like he fending off black flies, do an explanation part in English, part in sign language.

"Heap big chief come from…" and he stop and look at the interpreter man…"far off place where people only speak French?"

"Over the great water," say the man, waving his own arms, then staring around funny when he seen what he done.

"Heap big. Heap big," we all repeat, just like we was at a church service.

"How big is heap big?" says Robert Coyote.

"Bigger than a bus," says Bedelia Coyote.

"Undo your fly, Frank, and show them how big heap big is," says Frank's girl Connie.

But Frank is busy try to communicate this business of *over the water*. He make splashing motions, like putting soap all over himself, while we try to guess what he is doing.

"Putting on war paint?" says somebody.

"Wiping off a skunk smell," says somebody else.

We finally guess *over the water*.

"Does that mean Bittern Lake or the Saskatchewan River?" ask Connie Bigcharles.

"What is going on here?" ask Constable Chretien, puff out his chest like a partridge to show he is important.

"Tell the redcoat we don't speak no English here," I say to the interpreter in Cree.

If there was ever to be a Dumb Contest, Constable Chretien would win easy. He hardly speak the English and nobody around here speak French. His mouth hang open about three inches, and his eyes is focused off in the distance as he busy listening in French. Because of that Constable Chretien always be about a full minute behind what is happening around him.

The interpreter and the constable have a little pow-wow.

"Deze Indians is feeling particularly frisky today," says Constable Chretien.

"Heap big. Heap big. Over the water," we say.

The carload of suits all stand around stare at the sky as if they expect something to fall out of it.

We settle down and let them explain to us that it is Prince Philip who is the important visitor going to come to see us. From reading the papers it seem to me these royal people must sure hate the place where they live 'cause some of them are always in Canada, or Australia, or China. Weather must be really bad for them to want to get away so often. Prince Philip is the husband of the Queen of England, a man who walk around like he got his hands permanently tied behind his back. He always have his head bent forward like he is about to sniff a flower that is just out of the picture. He wear blue suits with medals stuck on his chest like so many scalps.

"His Royal Highness the Duke of Edinburgh is very interested in you native Canadians," says one of the suits.

"Yeah, well you tell him we're really interested in him too," says Bedelia. "Tell him we'd like him to do something typically *royal* while he's visiting us. You know, take a sponge bath, or teach us how to look down our noses at somebody."

"We are not amused," says the suit.

"Neither are we," says Bedelia. "Aren't you going to ask us to do something typically *Indian* while the Prince is here?"

"As a matter of fact..."

"Hey, how about we stage a buffalo hunt," yells Frank.

"Good idea, Fence-post," I say. And all of us dance along in a single line, sort of dragging our feet and pumping our arms. "We'll have a buffalo charge down the main street of Hobbema..."

"The only street in Hobbema," says Frank.

"And we'll have our best warriors ride him down and

kill him. Then we have a big buffalo barbecue in honour of the Prince."

"Barbecue. Barbecue," everybody say.

"Are you sure you're capable of doing this?" asks a suit.

"We do it all the time when there ain't no white men around to watch us," we say.

"Hey, Constable Chretien," says Rufus Firstrider, "who is this Duke that coming to visit?"

"Is he one of them Dukes of Hazzard?" says Frank.

"I hope it's the one with blond hair," says Connie Bigcharles. "Boy, he can dig his spurs in my flanks anytime."

"How soon did you say he was coming?" we ask.

"October 20th," say the sneakiest looking suit, who is small with a head like an egg, and silver-rimmed glasses that catch the sunshine and throw it around, "that's five weeks from now."

"How many moons is that?" we ask the Cree interpreter.

"Come on guys, haven't you put us on enough for one day?"

"No, really," we say.

"Okay, five weeks would be a moon and a quarter."

"Let's see," says Frank, "there's the moon of disappearing interpreters, the moon of dead RCMP constables, the moon of barbecued white men." Frank pretend to count on his fingers. "Right, October 20th," and he smile big.

"Barbecue. Barbecue," we all say.

Constable Chretien pull me and Frank off to one side. "Silas Ermineskin and Frank Fence-post, I will expect a buffalo hunt on the October 20th," and he look real serious at us, and I am beginning to think Constable Chretien understanding more than he used to, "if not, me and many redcoats come over the hills to visit you, and we look for much moonshine and many stolen car parts, and guess who the first two Indians we carry off to jail will be?" and he stop waving his arms around.

"Oui, Mesieur Constable," I say.

"Me too," says Frank.

The next day, when we get to thinking about what we agreed to do, we have second thoughts, and even third.

"Where are we gonna get a buffalo?" we ask each other.

"I think we should pretend we didn't understand what we was doing," says Eathen Firstrider. "That's always worked before."

Not understanding *has* always worked before. I remember a story Mr. Nicholls, my teacher and counsellor at the Tech School in Wetaskiwin tell me.

In the old days, right after the white man take all the Indians' land for himself, and give back to the Indians these little reservations, a group of important white men come to a reserve, try to explain to the Indians why they can only hunt on the reservation, because the land all around them either belong to farmers or is what they call Crown Land. The idea of someone owning land is foreign to Indians, but Crown Land is even stranger. The interpreter tries the best he can but Crown Land is awful hard to translate. A crown translate as the Queen's hat. So the best interpreter can do is explain to the Indians that the land all around their reserve is owned by the Queen's Hat.

The Indians talk that back and forth, shake their heads and laugh and laugh. They always knew the white men were crazy but to tell them that the great wilderness was now owned by the Queen's Hat was just too much.

Frank and me ain't too anxious to get charged with all the crimes going on around the reserve, so we argue for doing the buffalo hunt.

Everybody finally agree we will at least look for a buffalo.

"I heard of a rancher, live off east of Camrose, supposed to raise buffalo," says Robert Coyote.

Turns out that rancher live about 50 miles the other side of Camrose. He is named Mr. Lepage, and is a squinty-eyed old cowboy with tobacco-stained whiskers and a dirty cowboy hat, look like a horse chewed on it.

"He's so bowlegged you could graze a flock of sheep between his legs and nobody would notice," whispers Frank.

"Whatta you young bucks want with a buffalo anyway?" says Mr. Lepage, as we all walking along the side of a coulee a mile or so from his farm buildings.

I suppose it occurred to him that it is kind of funny for a bunch of Indians to be buying a buffalo from a white man.

"Prince Philip is coming all the way from England to Hobbema Reserve, and we promised to have a buffalo hunt in his honour," we say.

"I be go to hell," says Mr. Lepage. "Indians is gettin' crazier than white men. But if it's a buffalo you want, it's a buffalo you'll get." We walk for about another mile.

There is a couple of patches of red willow in the distance and it pretty hard to tell which is the willow stand and which is the buffalo. And neither one move as we get closer.

Turn out Mr. Lepage is exaggerating just a little. There is only one buffalo. The only other buffalo we ever seen was at the Alberta Game Farm, or in picture books. Even the ones in picture books looked more alive than this one. Only way we can tell it is alive is we can hear it breathing, kind of wheezing, like a cold wind blowing down the draw. Its eyes is glassy and its coat look like a lot of used mops been glued to its body.

"You sure he's alive?" asks Frank.

He look to me like he been taxidermied, and maybe got sticks on the other side of him propping him up.

"No wonder buffalos is extinct," says Bedelia Coyote.

"Where else you figure you goin' to find a buffalo?" asks Mr. Lepage, and he have a mean twinkle in his eye when he say it.

When he tell us how much he want in money we almost fall over.

"But he's old…and ragged…and sorrowful…" we say.

"Buffalos are in short supply," says Mr. Lepage.

"I bet buyers is too," says Eathen.

But Mr. Lepage stick to his price and we have to go searching for money.

First place we try is Chief Tom. We know Chief Tom will be hanging around like a big dog all the time Prince Philip is at the reserve. The Chief will stick his big face into every picture that get taken and will have to give a welcome speech last a half hour or longer.

"Well, young people, what can I do for you?" ask the Chief when we call on him at his apartment in Wetaskiwin, where he live with his girlfriend Samantha Yellowknees. Chief Tom he consider himself too white to live on the reserve no more.

We explain about the buffalo.

"No way," says Chief Tom.

"No buffalo, no barbecue," says Bedelia. "The Prince is gonna think you're pretty chintzy if you bring in food from Wetaskiwin."

About this time Samantha Yellowknees get in on the act. She is the brains behind Chief Tom. She pull the Chief off to one side and have a little talk to him, all the time making notes on the clipboard she always carry. "Bet she takes that thing to bed with her and makes notes on how Chief Tom can improve his lovemaking," whispers Bedelia.

Chief Tom come back to us, smiling like he just figured out how to cheat somebody. "Young people, we think you have a very good idea and on behalf of the Government of Alberta, the Constituency of Wetaskiwin…"

"Why don't you just skip the bullshit and give us the money," says Bedelia. Behind Chief Tom, Samantha make a mean little smile and wave a cheque in her fingers.

"We have decided that since there will be an official commemorative programme honouring the visit of His Royal Highness Prince Philip the Duke of Edinburgh," Chief Tom run right on, "we will have printed in said programme, 'Buffalo hunt sponsored by and wild buffalo donated by Chief Tom Crow-eye of the Ermineskin Band.'"

We all clap our hands.

"Is this a good quality buffalo?" asks Samantha.

"A-one-owner, Buffalo," says Frank.

"Only driven to pow-wows by a little old squaw," says Bedelia.

"We gonna name him Big Tom, after you," we tell the Chief, then we get out of there and head for the bank to cash the cheque before they ask many more questions.

Boy, we used to think it was tough to load Mad Etta, our medicine lady into the back of Louis Coyote's pick-up truck. That buffalo ain't very frisky, but he sure is stubborn. We first have to lead him all the way back to Mr. Lepage's corral where we have a loading chute. That buffalo sort of sway like he drunk as he walk and his joints creak like squeaky hinges. At the corral, me, Frank, Robert, Eathen, Rufus, and even the girls push on his backside to get him into the truck.

"Two thousand pounds of sadness," puffs Frank.

The buffalo make kind of a sad cry and break wind.

Back at the reserve we let the buffalo, what most of us call Little Etta, graze with Willard Wildman's horses a good mile back in the bush. Only it don't graze so much; it just stand like a brushpile, eyes closed, nose about an inch from the ground.

The day of the celebration come around before we know it. Early in the morning we push and pull the buffalo into town where we tether it behind Ben Stonebreaker's store. Not that it would be likely to go anywhere if we didn't tether it.

"Meanest buffalo since Confederation," we assure Chief Tom and Samantha.

Chief Tom have a special grandstand built at the end of Main Street, for him and Samantha, Premier Lougheed, Prince Philip and all the guys in suits and ties who accompany them. Constable Chretien stand at attention at the foot of that bleacher, what made out of lumber so new we can still smell the pine sap. Constable Chretien look stiff as a statue of an RCMP.

"They got wooden Indians," says Frank, "no reason why there can't be wooden RCMP's too."

Behind the store we all gather around the buffalo. What is happening right now is Carson Longhorn, Molly Thunder, my sister Delores and a bunch of other dancers is kicking up dust in front of that grandstand doing the Buffalo Dance. When that is over, Chief Tom, who already welcomed everybody for forty minutes, going to announce a surprise. "The Hobbema Chapter of the Ermineskin Warrior Society going to stage a live buffalo hunt right before our eyes," he will say. Then we supposed to release our buffalo and have him charge down the street. Robert Coyote, Eathen and Rufus Firstrider, and two other guys who know how to shoot with a bow and arrow, are all decked up like wild Indians, ride on pinto ponies we got from a riding academy in Ponoka. The guys who know how to use arrows are gonna kill our buffalo. Soon as it fall dead we got three big game hunters ready to carve it up. After that, the Blue Quills Ladies Auxiliary is waiting with a half dozen rented barbecues. They gonna cook up that buffalo and everybody have a feast.

Gerard Many Hands High, one of the hunters who going to kill the buffalo, stare down at it from his pony. All the hunters is mostly naked and smeared with war paint.

"Maybe if I ride up on him from behind real fast, I can make it look like he's moving," says Gerard. "It going to be like shooting arrows into a barn door."

We hear Chief Tom make the announcement. The hunters ride around the far side of the store and out onto the street. Their ponies prance around some. At the far end of the street we can see the grandstand and hear the murmur of the big crowd.

I pull on the halter. "Come on Little Etta, give us a run," I say, but all I get for an answer is a wheeze.

I lead him to the street and take off the halter. I at least get him pointed in the right direction. We all get behind him and start to yell and slap his rump. We hope he will at least take a few steps.

We all slap and yell.

"Maaaasmph," says the buffalo, take only one step before his left front leg crumple like it was made of jelly and the buffalo roll over almost in slow motion, lay on his side, sigh once, and be still, his eyes turned back in his head.

The hunting party ride up and look at the buffalo.

"Alright, which one of you guys shot him before he got a chance to run," says Frank.

I take Frank's arm and we start the long walk toward the grandstand. The hunting party ride behind us.

About half way there I beckon to Mad Etta, who standing on the side of the road and she join us. I figure people won't get so mad at us if we travelling with a 400 pound lady.

"First one who shoots an arrow at Etta going to be in a lot of trouble," she say to the hunting party, as she waddle along.

When we get in front of the new grandstand, I sort of raise up my hand, palm forward, the way people expect an Indian to.

"We're really sorry, Chief Tom," I say, "but our buffalo is dead."

"Dead?" say Chief Tom, and clap a hand to his forehead.

"Of natural causes," I say.

"Natural causes?" say the Chief into the microphone.

"Bad echo around here," says Frank.

"But the hunt...the barbecue..." says the Chief.

"Buffalo died of boredom, listening to him welcome everybody," says Mad Etta, just loud enough for me and Frank to hear.

"You can send for the coroner if you like," says Frank. "We didn't have nothing to do with it."

Chief Tom sputtering into the microphone as his head been held under water for quite a while.

Boy, I am close enough to see that this here Prince is a real person. He wearing a Navy uniform with gold braid and medals.

"I bet he could be captain of *The Love Boat* if he wanted to," says Frank.

Prince Philip stand up and walk down the steps toward us. About a dozen suits move from the stage and from under the grandstand and almost form a circle around him. The Prince move right along toward the hunting party though, reach up his hand toward Gerard Many Hands High, and ask him about the lance Gerard is carrying.

On stage, Chief Tom is still sputtering.

Constable Chretien look at me and Frank like one of us just spit on his boots.

"I don't suppose we could drive to Wetaskiwin and get a few buckets of Kentucky Fried Chicken," I say. "The ladies down at Blue Quills cooked up bannock and sas-

katoon pie to go with the buffalo." But nobody answer
me.

Constable Chretien stare us down with an expression
that say, "Just you wait," and I guess that is about all we
got to do right now.

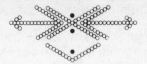

THE MOTHER'S
DANCE

RUFUS FIRSTRIDER sit cross-legged in the middle of the floor at Blue Quills Hall, bang on his drum. The dancers, both men and women, shuffle around Rufus in a wide circle, their moccasins gliding over the smooth yellow hardwood. Each one of them dancers hold a baby, either their own or borrowed, anywhere from brand new to a year or so old. As they shuffle to the beat of the drum, the dancers hold them babies way up high, as if they was pushing them toward the sun. Some of the babies giggle, some of the babies cry, and some keep right on with their sleeping.

Sometimes the Government make me so mad I get tears in my eyes just from thinking of what they done, or try to do to us Indians.

It was about two years ago in April that we know something bad going down because a carload of guys from the Indian Affairs Department in Edmonton come sneak around the reserve ask funny questions like, "How many families is named Coyote? How many families is named Small Grey Eyes?" They ask about more than just those two families. I think we counted over ten altogether, and they want to know, "Who was the grandfather? Who was the great-grandfather?" They snoop all the way back to the time the reserve was formed and even before.

We tell them mainly lies and try to confuse them. We found out a long time ago that if we tell the Government the truth, no matter how simple the question, they find a way to either charge us money, or take away something that already belongs to us.

"Coyote family all painted their skins white by jumping in a barrel of flour and water, joined the Mormon Church, and been off attending Mormon Family Night at the Calgary Stampede for must be two or three years now," Frank Fence-post tells them investigators.

"We beginning to suspect they not coming home no more," Bedelia Coyote tell them real seriously. The Government men never bat any kind of smile; they just write everything down on the black clipboards they carry.

This time, what the Government has decided to do is make white people out of about a dozen families, or at least they decide these families can't be Indian no more. All the Department is worried about is maybe these people be living on the reserve illegally. They got no care for what becomes of the people. After they sneak around investigating for almost a year they give them dozen families notice that they got sixty days to pack up and leave the reserve for good.

What cause the trouble in the first place was that some civil servant, digging for whatever reason in dusty old records in Ottawa, come up with some papers what show that when the Hobbema Reserve was formed, quite a few families of Indians choose not to live on the reserve. The head of each one of them families was given a piece of *scrip*, what entitle them to a quarter-section of farm land. But when an Indian take that scrip it mean that forever and always him or his family don't be allowed to live on the reserve.

I went and look scrip up in the dictionary at the Tech School in Wetaskiwin, and it mean "A certificate of a right to receive something." That look to be correct with the story. At least the Government got that part right.

But what happen is the Indians who get that scrip don't have any idea what it means. Them Indians still lived in teepees and hunted buffalo. They don't understand the white man's idea of selling the land on which the people walk. Lots of Indians still don't understand.

Some smart white men come along and buy up that scrip from the Indians for a little money, a few blankets, or a bucket of whisky. When we finally get around to checking things out, we find of fifteen families been given that scrip, only two ever claimed the land, and only one, my friend Old Joe Buffalo ever farmed it.

When that civil servant in Ottawa pull out that paper he get the bright idea of checking the Hobbema Reserve to see if any of them families sneaked back and is living where they not supposed to be.

Some of the people who get notices that they have to move are the Coyotes, the Moses Cardinals, the Strong-eagles, the Small Grey Eyes, and the Stonechilds. One or two of the names like Drifting Cloud, and Rosebud, ain't known around Hobbema no more.

This here scrip was given out close to a hundred years ago, so if a family lived illegally on the reserve for all that time, there get to be quite a few people involved. Bedelia Coyote counted them all up and found there was over 300, that be almost 10% of all the Indians live at Hobbema.

"What do they mean we got to leave the reserve?" Blind Louis Coyote say when Bedelia read the letter been sent to him by registered mail. Louis been blind for a lot of years and he lived all his life on the reserve, have enough relatives around make a tribe of their own.

It sure sad to see so many people running from place to place, each one asking the other, "What can we do?"

My friend Bedelia Coyote do the best she can. She is one of the ones told to go, and she is also a person like to fight with the Government every chance she get. And Bedelia is a tough person to tangle with. But everywhere she go she get nothing but runarounds. She bang her fist up against the wall at her cabin one night. "I feel like there's a foot-thick glass wall between me and all these figureheads I talk to. They see me but they don't hear me." Bedelia is short and stocky, walk with her head down and like she know where she is going. She usually wear jeans and a thick green sweater with a turtle neck. She have a soft, flat nose, and deep set eyes, her hair is parted down the middle so when I look at it from above it look like a white line been painted on her head.

First thing Bedelia do is organize a meeting at Blue Quills Hall of all the people been told to move on. So many people get after Chief Tom Crow-eye that he comes to the meeting himself, all dressed up in his Conservative-blue suit and silk tie.

"I've studied up on these here papers," he say in his oily voice. It is a voice he learned after he took a public speaking course in Edmonton. Chief Tom is not only our chief, but he is the local representative for Premier Lougheed's Government. So we have to put most of our hopes on him. "It look to me," he go on, "like the government got itself a pretty good case. These people was paid to leave the reserve forever. I think you are pretty lucky that the government don't try to collect for the benefits they paid you for so many years. Only thing I can think of to do is ask the Provincial Government for some money to help you relocate. I bring it up at the next session of the Legislature…"

"If it were your friends getting kicked out instead of mainly people who vote against you, you'd do something," yell Bedelia.

"Yeah," says Mad Etta our medicine lady, "what if the Crow-eye name was on that list?"

"But it wasn't," says Chief Tom, and he can't help

smirking just a little. "The Crow-eyes have always been law abiding and loyal..."

"Apples..." call out Bedelia.

Wouldn't matter much to Chief Tom if he did get kicked off the reserve; couple of years ago he left his wife and gone to live in an apartment in Wetaskiwin with his girlfriend, Samantha Yellowknees.

"Now, my friends, I know it seems unfair at the moment but one has to consider the government's position. They dispensed land in good faith..."

"We can't be penalized for something that was done in ignorance by our grandfathers," says Bedelia.

"We cannot be selective in obeying laws," says Chief Tom. "If some treaties and agreements are valid, then all are valid."

"Where are we going to go?" people keep asking, but nobody got an answer. Everybody get to say their piece, but Chief Tom field them questions like he was batting away beach balls. It become plain to see nobody gonna get no help from him.

As we leaving the hall I see Mary Small Grey Eyes sitting on a yellow folding chair, her shoulders shaking.

"I got no place to go," she says in Cree, and grabs onto my sleeve. Mary is about 70 and look like a real scrawny tree been covered with a tan-coloured coat, got half its buttons missing. Mary's husband, Archie Small Grey Eyes, died a few years ago and her kids gone off to the city. To top it off, she was born a Dodginghorse, and only *married* into one of the "illegal" families. But the Government say everyone who carry the name got to leave.

Her face got a desperate look about it. I try to think of something nice to say to her but can't come up with anything. Instead, I walk her back to her cabin and hang around until she get her coal-oil lamp lit.

"It's like shooting at the sky for raining on you," says Bedelia. "There's nobody to fight, no necks I can get my hands around."

"Maybe if we was to get a lawyer," I suggest.

Some of us go to the Legal Aid place in Edmonton. The lawyers is nice, but what they really say is there ain't no point in fighting the Government. "Besides," they say, "it could take years of studying the law to present a proper case, and besides, who would pay us?"

"We all for having the case drag on for years," we tell them.

"Maybe you could get the government to help with relocation costs," they suggest.

The day for the moving comes up on us fast. As a last resort we try to get the newspapers to carry the story. Bedelia Coyote know from reading *MS. Magazine* and from all her business with the Women for Equality and outfits like that, how to write a "press release." We mail the story off to quite a few papers and carry it to the *Wetaskiwin Times* and the *Edmonton Journal.* At both those papers the reporters smile nice and say they'll think about it.

"Some white man get his spare tire stolen and it make the front page," say Bedelia. "Maybe if somebody got killed or if we had a picture of a girl in a shoe-lace bathing suit to go with the story."

Bedelia don't know then how right she is.

Mary Small Grey Eyes couldn't wait for that moving day to get no closer. She is just an old lady don't understand why white men want to move her away from the home she known all her life. She hang herself from a poplar limb, using a soft-drink case as a step so she can stand on top of a cream can, tie a couple lengths of binder-twine around her neck.

"I hate to say this," Bedelia say when I tell her what Mary done, "but maybe now we get our story heard." And she call up the RCMP, the coroner in Wetaskiwin, Chief Tom Crow-eye, and them newspapers and TV stations in Edmonton.

The *Edmonton Journal* run a story and a picture of

Mary Small Grey Eyes, from the days when her name was Dodginghorse and she was a champion pow-wow dancer. The headline read:

SUICIDE BLAMED ON
GOVERNMENT DECISION

After that, stories about Mary's suicide make all the newspapers, and we have reporters crawling all around the reserve. They write follow-up stories about some of the families who are going to be put out of their homes. They run a picture of Blind Louis Coyote and his family, with Louis sitting on a broken-backed kitchen chair, his hands clasped on his white cane, his milky eyes staring off into the distance. The stories all mention Mary's suicide and how the suicide rate here at Hobbema is 1500% as high as for the whole province.

"Not a bad place to get kicked out of," says Frank Fence-post when I read that story to him. Most of those suicides is young people though, and have to do with drinking, drugs like angel dust, and kids sniffing glue or gasoline.

"Even a bad place is better than none," Mad Etta tell Frank.

The Government in Ottawa finally say they going to review the case, so they postpone the moving day for three months. It get talked about in the Parliament and the Legislature in Edmonton. The Minister of Indian Affairs have to fly out here to Alberta to defend himself.

He be a fat man who think in French so his English always come out backside-foremost. He just makes a couple of speeches defending what the Government doing, and since he is the man who make the final decision we know how it going to come out.

In happier times, the Stony Indians up by Edmonton made that Minister an Honorary Chief. They say they is so mad at what being done to our Indians that they hold another ceremony and take back his appointment. They dance the ceremony dance backwards, and when they finished they burn a replica of the headdress they tied on him. That pretty good coming from the Stonys. They is a rich tribe, have oil on their reserve. They live in four-bedroom houses and drive Chryslers. "A whole reserve-full of Chief Toms," is how Mad Etta describe them once. "I forgot more about being Indian than they ever know," Etta say.

Finally, the announcement come, like we all knew it would, them families still got to move.

We have a final meeting, even though it seem every alternative been covered. The people who sit around on yellow folding chairs, on the basketball court at Blue Quills, are mainly families. The women, and even some of the men, all seem to be holding babies—look like everyone from fourteen or so on be in charge of some kind of baby: babies tiny as kittens with only little brown faces showing from a pink or blue blanket; babies big enough to wiggle, each wrapped in blankets or sleepers; and babies of a year or so, standing up on someone's knee by holding onto a finger, dressed in snowsuits, maybe wearing moccasins or baby-sized cowboy boots, stretching out, reaching curious hands toward the lights in the ceiling.

Bedelia ask Mad Etta to speak, and I don't know if Etta smell something in the air or not, but she tell a story that meant to give people hope, and Etta don't usually give hope unless there is a reason.

"An old man get to the Happy Hunting Grounds and meet up with the Manitou," Etta say. "The Manitou let the old man look back down here to earth where he can see all the trails he walked in his long life. The old man see that most all of his life there was two sets of foot-prints, one his, one the Manitou's. What puzzle the old man is that the places where there was only one set of prints was during the real bad times in his life. 'How come' the old man asks the Manitou, 'you left me alone when life was toughest?'

"'Ah, old friend,' said the Manitou, 'I didn't desert you in your times of need. The reason you see only one set of footprints is that those were the times when I was carrying you.'"

A few days later, when things get to their lowest point, so low that Mr. and Mrs. Blind Louis is packing up their furniture on the back of their old pickup truck; something happen, that if we was religious could be called a miracle. But since we ain't religious, it is more like something Mr. Nichols talked about in class. In English class he say how the ancient Greeks, when they wrote and put on plays, sometimes got their characters into bad and complicated situations that no author or actor could straighten out. What them Greeks did when they got themselves into a corner was have a fellow in a bedsheet climb down a rope from the rafters and land right in the middle of the play. This guy in the sheet was a god, and he solved all the problems just by pointing at different actors and saying things like, "You two are going to get married and live happily ever after," or, "You are going to get killed for being so nasty," or, "You will become king and make your people happy for many years." This god had a name that sounded like *Daze Exmacinaw,* but I never did see how it was spelled.

Like one of them gods from a Greek play or an angel of mercy, like they always writing about in the Bible, a lady from Calgary take up our cause. Her name is Grace McGee, which ain't an Indian name, but she is Indian, at least by birth. She been born on the Blood reserve down near the U.S. border, and her real name was Grace Many Hands High, until she married with a white man named McGee.

She read about Mary in the newspapers, and when our last appeal fail, she drive all the way to Hobbema in a car so long and black it look like it belong in a funeral line. We expect maybe someone like Premier Lougheed going to get out from behind the blue-tinted glass of the back windows. In the driver's seat is a man wearing a uniform and a leather hat.

The woman who climb out can't weigh more than 90 pounds. She wearing a brown fur jacket and black slacks. She is over 50, but how far over is hard to tll. Her face is the colour of tobacco; her eyes close together and deep set, and when she walk she don't totter on her high heels like we would expect, but plant them heels down firm in the dirt, leave little tracks the size of dimes in the damp earth.

"I want to see Bedelia Coyote," is the first thing she say to anybody, and she say it in Cree. I never knew Indian ladies could be as rich as this one.

We take her over to the Coyote's cabin.

"Unpack your stuff," she tell Blind Louis. "I've already got an injunction before the courts. You won't have to move anywhere unless you want to."

I have to look up the word *injunction*. It come through the next day, and near as I can figure it is kind of like temporarily damming a river.

That little Indian lady work like a whirlwind. She gather together all the people who supposed to be evicted. She talk to each family and make up charts show their history right back to the time the scrip was given out.

And little by little she let out bits of information about herself. Like she got a degree that make her a lawyer but until now she never used it for nothing. "I sat at home and had a houseful of kids," she tells us. "My husband makes all kinds of money so I don't have to work. My last daughter had gone away to university herself when I read about Mary Small Grey Eyes and what the government is trying to do to you people."

A few of us go up to Edmonton and sit in the small varnishy-smelling courtroom where the case be heard.

Mrs. McGee have a lot to say for herself and so do the sad looking Government lawyers, but it might as well be in some really foreign language for all we understand. The case drag on for three months and we get tired of sitting around, but we there the day the judge give his decision. We don't understand that either, but we can tell by the way Mrs. McGee jump up and down, smile, clasp her hands together, look up at us and give us the high sign, that everything turn out okay.

After the court case been won, things settle down to normal on the reserve, except everyone would like to say thank you, in some special way, to Grace McGee. Couple of times while she was working for us, we suggested that we hold a dance at Blue Quills Hall to raise money.

"No," she says, "I'm doing this for the Indian people. I'm lucky to have enough money that I don't have to worry about money." I sure wonder what that would be like. I know she tell the truth, because once a bunch of us went to her house in Calgary, and boy, it be big enough for a small hotel, got fancy furniture, and expensive paintings on the walls.

Still, we want to do something for her.

"We could go ahead raise some money, buy her something," Rufus Firstrider say.

"Like what?" I say. "Everything she own be more expensive than we can afford."

"There's got to be a better way," say Bedelia Coyote.

It is then that I remember the way little Mrs. McGee moved around the courtroom: how without even knowing it there was rhythm in the way she walked, shuffled actually. What she was doing was a dance, as she moved from behind her table, around the tables where the Government lawyers sat, then glided back and forth in front of the place where the judge sat way up high like a black bird on a post. She had on a bright green blouse with long sleeves and a high neck what was closed up tight by an arrowhead brooch. She wore a buckskin skirt that skimmed about a half-inch above the floor. I couldn't see her feet, but she moved in time to the rhythm of her voice, which, whether she knew it or not, was a chant. I think she might have even hypnotized that judge with her soft, even voice, or at least relaxed him.

"Why not create a dance for her?" I said, and it surprise me to hear my voice saying that.

"That's something a rich person can't buy," says Frank Fence-post.

And that's what we done. We get Carson Longhorn, who be the best chicken dancer in Alberta, to set the thing up. But we don't use any of the real dancers. The different womens' societies on the reserve have a meeting and decide to create that new dance in honour of Grace McGee. They decide to call it the Mother's Dance.

Mrs. McGee been invited for a month from now and she's accepted. I was down last night to Blue Quills to watch the practice.

Rufus Firstrider sit cross-legged in the middle of the floor at Blue Quills Hall, bang on his drum. The dancers, both men and women, shuffle around Rufus in a wide circle, their moccasins gliding over the smooth yellow hardwood. Each one of them dancers hold a baby, either their own or borrowed, anywhere from brand new to a year or so old. As they shuffle to the beat of the drum, the dancers hold them babies way up high, as if they was pushing them toward the sun. Some of the babies giggle, some of the babies cry, and some keep right on with their sleeping.

PIUS BLINDMAN
IS COMING
HOME

THE TROUBLE STARTED because Minnie Blindman's daughter told a lie. Betty, the daughter, got to be sixty or more years old. Her own family growed up and gone and her husband he died, must be close to ten years ago.

Betty, she checked first with her church to see if the lie was okay. After her husband died she got hooked in by one of the big churches in Wetaskiwin who like to have an Indian or two around to show they ain't prejudiced. Betty Thomas is big and flabby, wear thick glasses, grey dresses, and like to clasp her hands across her belly when she sitting down, and smile off into the distance like she sees something there that nobody else does.

The reason she told the lie was that the doctor say her mama is gonna die at any minute. Betty go around the reserve, all puffy-faced from crying and tell anybody who listen how much she loves her mama and how the old lady is the only reason she got for living.

"Sometimes if you love somebody you show it by letting them die," growl Mad Etta, after Betty been at Etta's cabin all afternoon, crying in her tea cup. "Nature know what its doing. That old lady so small she gonna get blown away by the wind just like a dried up leaf."

167

"I ask the reverend," Betty Thomas tell everyone, "and he said if it give Mama hope and make her live longer, then it is all right." I heard her say that myself one afternoon down to Blue Quills Hall. That must have been five years ago or more, and I bet her mama then was close to ninety.

The lie Betty Thomas told the old lady was that her son, Betty's brother, Pius Blindman, was coming home. Betty didn't even know where Pius Blindman was. Nobody did. But he was always the old lady's favourite and Betty figured to cheer her up.

"Pius phoned from over the mountains in British Columbia, I told Mama, say he catching the bus and he here in a few days."

After she heard that news from Betty, they say Old Minnie Blindman perk up like a wilted plant that been watered. She ain't done much for the last few years but lay on the black and white striped mattress on the old iron bed in Betty's cabin. Her mind, folks say, is pretty sharp, though she's not always sure about which is the past and which is right now. It is her body that is in bad shape, wearing down with the old age like a stone in a riverbed.

She have some kind of operation in the hospital in Wetaskiwin, and afterwards the doctors say for Betty to take her home to die.

I remember seeing Minnie Blindman a few times as she hobbled across Betty's yard. Old woman remind me of a small, spiky tree covered with grey-speckled cloth. She walk with a cane, scuffing up dust and scattering Betty's few orange-eyed Leghorns. She talk to herself in Cree and point a knobby old finger at us kids. She say things that don't make too much sense to us—tell us to grow up to be good strong hunters and say sometime she show us the best places in the hills to pick saskatoons.

The way Betty tell it, when Old Minnie hear that Pius Blindman is coming home, she raise herself up in bed and eat some solid food for the first time since she come from the hospital. Then she ask to get out of her nightgown and have her dress put on her. And she ask Betty to comb her hair for her, say it is 'cause she want to look nice for Pius, and she even shape her toothless old mouth, look like it been closed by a drawstring, into a smile.

There weren't nothing special about Pius Blindman except he was Minnie's only son. He would be fifty years old or so. I remember him as a thin, stoop-shouldered man with mean eyes. Once I seen him wear a yellow flannel shirt full of green lines look like oat stems been laid in square patterns on it. That is the way I see him in my mind. He sometime cut brush for the railway, but mostly did nothing at all. He hang around the bars in Wetaskiwin and Edmonton, and marry a city girl but don't stay with her long. She was about as bad as him and their kids got gived to the Welfare to raise. At the time Betty told the lie nobody around Hobbema had seen Pius for maybe five years. I read somewhere that families are groups of people that nobody else wants— guess that must be true—otherwise why would Old Minnie care about seeing Pius again?

If instead of her preacher Betty had asked somebody who knew what they was doing, somebody like Mad Etta our medicine lady who know more than any priest or doctor you can name; she would of been told not to tell the lie. Not because it was a lie, but because of what it would do to Old Minnie.

"There's a fat difference between giving out hope and giving out false hope," Mad Etta say to me. Etta is sitting on her tree-trunk chair in her cabin. It is hot September and the cabin is full of flies. Mad Etta wave them off her with her beefy big hand, but they just circle around and land where they was before.

Whatever the doctors thought was gonna kill Minnie Blindman, didn't. They were sure surprised when a week after Betty told the lie, that old woman was able to walk from the car into their office. In the office she grinned at them out of her thin, leathery face, as she talked Cree to Betty, answering the doctor's questions. "I'm better because my son Pius is coming home," she told Betty to tell them.

But it wasn't long before Old Minnie was sick again. "Nature knows what its doing," Etta said again, after she'd doctored some on the old woman. "Bodies wear out, just like clothes or cars, ain't nothing me or anybody else can do for her."

But we all, even Etta, didn't guess at how deep and hot the fire was that kept Minnie Blindman alive and looking forward to seeing her son.

She have at least one or two operations every year since then. Doctors have to open her up again and again, rearrange her insides. They take out parts she don't need and patch up what's left.

Two years ago her circulation go bad and one of her legs have to come off above the knee. Betty get the preacher from church down to the hospital that time and they pray over her for a while. Betty Thomas she signed the old lady up to the church, not because Old Minnie have any idea of what she is doing, but because it make Betty feel more righteous than she is already. Doctors only do that leg operation because Betty insist. They say no way the old woman's heart can stand the shock.

But she keep on living. There is kind of a haze between her and the world. She don't realize how much time has gone by. To her it is like only a day or so has passed since she heard Pius was coming home. Every day she thinks is going to be that day. And the thought of it, like a strong medicine, keeps her alive.

Last winter she go into the hospital again and have her right eye taken out because doctors say she got cancer in there. Her eyelid is fallen in, look like a brown leaf been pushed in where the eye used to be. When she get home, my friend Eathen Firstrider, he wire up boards along each side of her bed so she can't fall off to the floor. All day, every day, she lay mainly on her back, like a baby, her old tobacco-coloured hands waving slowly in front of her face. The big veins on the backs of her hands are the colour of new denim.

Minnie get so she have to have a babysitter, just like she was a child, and my girlfriend, Sadie One-wound, take on the job some evenings. Old Minnie have to be kept in diapers, and the cabin full of the smell of soiled cloth and sour milk. Sadie have to change those diapers. When she do I try to look the other way. It is like my eyes was metal and a magnet keep pull them over toward the bed. The old lady's thighs and belly covered in red, pusy-looking sores—she have a disease the doctors call *shingles*. When I look at her, even when I'm across the room my stomach come up in my throat. I couldn't do things like that for a growed up person.

But on those evenings when I visit, even as sick as she is, when she hears a man's voice, Old Minnie raise up her head and whisper, "Pius, is that you? Have you come home?"

"It's only my boyfriend," Sadie tells her. The old lady drops her head back on her pillow and goes to sleep.

It was maybe a month ago that Betty come to Etta's cabin. Etta and me was playing rummy with a deck missing two cards. Etta cheats if you don't watch her close. But she says cheating is part of the game; it teach you keep your eyes open and watch your opponent.

"I can't take no more," Betty says. "That thing over there that *was* my mama is never gonna die."

Etta stay silent and look Betty up and down. If ever Etta have the chance to say "I told you so," this is it. But she don't take it.

"Why are you telling me?" says Etta. "You told her the lie. You untell it."

"Etta, you got to tell her."

"Get your god-man to do it."

"He don't speak no Cree. Never been out to the reserve either."

"Make it easy for him to give advice then, don't it?"

"Please, Etta." Betty Thomas' glasses are fogging up. Tears ooze out from under the glass and make paths down her fat cheeks.

"She'll die if you tell her," says Etta. "It will be just like turning out a light. Who wants that responsibility? You sure ain't ready for it or you wouldn't be here."

Betty Thomas get kind of snooty after that, act as if Etta is at fault for not jumping up quick to do the dirty work. But finally she go away, sniffling loud.

Next day I suggest to some of the guys down at the pool hall at Hobbema that maybe *we* could find Pius Blindman and bring him home to see his mama.

"We'll be just like some of them detectives on TV," says my friend Frank Fence-post. Frank he square up his shoulders and say he pretend he is this *Magnum PI* fellow. "We have lots of pretty girls hang all over us, a fancy car, we get in lots of fist fights and win them all, and always make the cops look like jerks."

"That only happens on TV," I say. And I don't know then how right I am.

"How do we go about finding a guy nobody has seen for ten years," we ask, and don't come up with too many answers. Nobody we know of have a picture of Pius. We suppose police in Wetaskiwin and Edmonton do, but they sure wouldn't give it out to us even if we told them we was doing detective work.

We take Louis Coyote's truck and drive up to Edmonton where we check out the Indian bars: the York, the New Empire, the Royal, the Hub, and a couple of others, but we don't find no sign of Pius Blindman. We check too around the Sally Ann, the Single Men's Shelter, and a couple of Missions, without having any better luck.

Then, just by looking in the Edmonton telephone book

we find a listing for a Jeannie Blindman who turn out to be Pius' exwife. She ain't a very nice lady. She got a voice like a rasp grating on iron, and all she have to say about him is, "When that S.O.B. dies, I hope he dies slow." We find out that we seen him since she has.

We do that same kind of check of bars and shelters in Red Deer and Calgary. We make us some pretty good parties while we checking the bars but we don't find out nothing about Pius Blindman.

Finally, I go see the RCMP in Wetaskiwin. Most RCMP's is young and like to bang their boots on the floor when they walk.

"You want to file a Missing Persons Report?" a young officer with short hair and a square chin say to me.

"I guess."

"What kind of relative is he?"

"He's Betty Thomas' brother and Minnie Blindman's son, and…"

"No. No. How is he related to you?"

"He ain't."

"Why do you want to find him? He owe you money?" and the young constable grin at me like he just said something smart. "You can't file a Missing Persons Report unless you're a relative."

"His old Mama want to see him before she die."

"How long's he been gone?"

"Ten years or so."

"Ten years!" the constable say in a loud voice. "You'd better have his mother or some blood relative come in and file the report."

The next time I see Constable Greer driving his patrol car down the street, I flag him down. Constable Greer is an old RCMP. "They're gonna leave me here in Wetaskiwin until I retire," he told us once. Constable Greer is too nice to be an RCMP; I guess that is why he never get promoted.

When I tell him my story he say he'll have a look in the

files and see what he can do for us. "But don't come around the office asking questions. I'll let you know what I find out."

About three months later Constable Greer pull his car up to the curb just as me and Frank Fence-post and our girlfriends Sadie One-wound and Connie Bigcharles is coming out of the Alice Hotel.

Constable Greer say that the RCMP's finally link up Pius Blindman's fingerprints from the times he got picked up drunk in Wetaskiwin, to the prints of a man who got killed walking down the shoulder of the Trans-Canada Highway, near a place called Ignace, Ontario. That happen six, maybe seven years ago. "He was buried as a John Doe," Constable Greer say. No one knew what Pius Blindman was doing there, so far from home.

Sadie still babysit for Betty Thomas. Once in a while old Minnie Blindman speak up in Cree, don't care if anybody listening or not. Her one eye from the dark of the bed look like it belong to an animal hid deep in a hedge. "Even He died," she say one night, and I see she looking at a crucifix what Betty hung from the wood railing that make the bed into a crib. "I can't die," she wail, and her rusty old voice get louder than I ever imagined it could. "I can't die until Pius gets here. He's on his way. I can't die until I see him again." Then she make little whimpering sounds like a baby, and curl up, pulling her one leg up under her chin. She is frail as willow twigs and tiny as a four year old.

Last night Sadie walk down to the Hobbema General Store for cigarettes, leave me alone with the old woman. Sadie is hardly gone when Old Minnie wake up making sobbing sounds like maybe she was having a bad dream.

"It's all right," I say. "You're not alone."

"Pius, is that you?" she say real clear, and stare over in my direction. She pull her head onto her pillow, and brush her hair off her face just like a school girl.

I move one step deeper into the shadows. In the orange glow of the coal oil lamp Minnie's one eye glows red, tiny and full of hate as a wolverine in a trap. I stand real still. My shadow is tall and black and folds over the middle of the bed and up the wall.

"Pius, is that you?" the old woman says again.

I guess it don't even make no sense for me to what him

punished. He was asking for it all along. I guess I been

been in jail long enough now. My old MP came down to

see me already show that and above him, but he was

charged with murder even though I never no. He been

a bundled whole show. It got is been over any more

was 40 and I says up to him.

Bad times around this. The papers going around

the city. I know what they are up it. I release Court

Murdine that the papers for the trouble. Be the

founder of CHP that has redone the Provost

Crow that off to the City to war I was the Assembly

Indian. I know many people and been what times in the

last year so made the head of the that took had but look

stupid.

That I guess was his worst mistake. Your enemies

never like to be made look stupid. Clover have the law

vote for CHP take the CHP because. What they do

them lawyers show that the MP and you bring

through their teeth, while everyone know the trouble

time when it comes to cases where Indians is in trouble

but that they plan their hopes that it and just, the

FUGITIVES

I GUESS NOBODY ever going to know for sure what happened one afternoon in June 1977 at the Red Pheasant Reserve in Saskatchewan. Two RCMP guys ended up dead, everybody know that. And Grover Manybears got charged with murder, even though there must have been a hundred or more shots fired on both sides and there was 40 or 50 guys with guns.

That June afternoon the RCMP come snooping around the reserve for no good reason except to hassle Grover Manybears and his friends because Grover be the founder of CIFF, Canadian Indians For Freedom. Grover been off to the USA to study with the American Indian Movement people, and quite a few times in the last year he made the RCMP not just look bad, but look stupid.

That I guess was his worst mistake. Your enemies never like to be made look stupid. Grover have the lawyers for CIFF take the RCMP to court. When they do, them lawyers show that the RCMP not just lying through their teeth, which everyone know they do all the time when it comes to cases where Indians is in trouble, but that they plan their lies, and that it ain't just the constables who make the arrests who lying, but their bosses in Regina and Saskatoon, men who knew all about the lies and okayed them.

After Grover Manybears and the lawyers from CIFF bring in new evidence and witnesses, why quite a few people get new trials and is acquitted, and a whole lot of cases due to come to trial was just dropped. A couple of junior constables get fired for lying, and the head Inspector of RCMP's for the Red Pheasant area suddenly get transferred to Quebec.

After that, Grover go on a speaking tour of other reserves in Saskatchewan and Alberta tell how he defeat the RCMP at their own sneaky games.

Grover Manybears is stocky built, got a little tummy that hang over his belt. He is about 35, have long black hair to below his shoulders, brown eyes, a large fleshy nose, and a brush of a moustache that cover his upper lip completely. Grover always wear a red bandana tied across his forehead just like a pirate; that bandana tied so low it cover up his eyebrows.

The RCMP aren't quick to forget when someone make them look like fools, and they start to follow Grover around. Wherever he talk, why the RCMP don't interfere with his speech, but they set up roadblocks and search all the cars and trucks coming to his meeting, and all those they find parked anywhere around the meeting house. They issue tickets for every little thing, like having license plate lights burned out, or tires without enough tread. They check for unpaid traffic tickets, expired insurance cards and stuff like that, then they arrest the drivers and carry them off to jail. They even give tickets for not using seat belts, a law that ain't enforced anywhere else in the province. Grover's lawyers get most of the charges dropped, but it get so people hate to take the trouble to come hear him.

The shooting started at a pow-wow, when the RCMP come along with a whole van-load of young constables just graduate the RCMP school in Regina. These guys ain't even in uniform, just got a badge in their pocket to show they is policemen.

One of these young policemen give a ticket to a man named Louis Heifer because the back end of Louis' pickup is jacked up one inch higher than some silly law say it ought to be. Louis tear up the ticket, get in his truck and drive off. The constable call out that Louis is under arrest, take a gun from his jacket and go to shoot at the back of the truck. Somebody knock the gun from his hand and it shoot into the ground. Pretty soon everybody is running for their guns and the Indians and RCMP draw up lines and shoot at each other for most of an hour. Two of them young constables get shot.

About three days later the RCMP charge Grover Manybears with both murders.

They have the trial in Regina in front of a white jury. All they got is one witness, a scrawny little Indian woman with eyes tiny as drill points. Her name is Anna Wolverine and she don't speak English. The RCMP bring in a Cree-speaking person all the way from Ottawa to deliver Anna Wolverine's words.

What she say is: "When the shooting start I hid under my old man's truck. Grover Manybears was there with a big rifle and he was shooting. I seen him hit two of the men across the clearing."

Grover have the CIFF lawyers working for him. They bring in lots of witnesses and they try really hard for him, but the one thing they can't do is break Anna Wolverine's story. She really sound like a lady who is telling the truth.

The jury only take an hour to find Grover guilty and he get sentenced to two life terms in prison.

You can bet every RCMP in the country smile big when they hear that. What they don't count on is Grover being slippery as a live fish. Before they can even move him to the big prison at Prince Albert, Grover escape. He manage to stay free for eleven days before he get caught hitch-hiking toward US border.

Grover's lawyers file every kind of appeal possible and they keep on trying to find new evidence that would set Grover Manybears free. Part of the new evidence is that two other Indians, Bill Wildcat and Mose Gauthier, come forward to say they was the ones who shot the RCMP's. They even tell how they dumped their rifles in a lake way back on the reserve.

The RCMP's sent out a team to drag the lake; they find the guns and haul them away, but then nothing happen. When Grover's lawyers ask about the guns the RCMP claim they never sent no one to the lake. They claim they don't believe the stories of Bill Wildcat and Mose Gauthier.

Then one day Anna Wolverine come to see Grover's lawyers.

"I lied," she say. "I never saw nothing that day. But the social workers come around my house the next week say they going to take my kids away from me. We ain't no worse off than anybody else, but they say there been complaints about my old man roughing up the kids, and about us not having enough food, and the house not being insulated. Social workers say they going to take my kids away to the city and I never see them again.

"Next day," she say, "the RCMP come around tell me if I testify against Grover Manybears they fix it so I can keep my kids. What else could I do?"

Grover's lawyers take an official statement from Anna and send it to the Attorney General of Saskatchewan, the Justice Department in Ottawa, and anybody else who should be interested in justice.

Indians, and even some white people, is plenty upset by what happened. There is meetings to plan action, people sign petitions for Grover to get a new trial.

There is even some bumper stickers printed up that read: FREE GROVER MANYBEARS.

Grover's girlfriend, Sandra Burn, is the one who do a lot of that organizing, write letters and press releases, keep the pressure on the courts and the Government. Sandra is one pretty woman. Not so much pretty as proud. Everything about her is straight and tough. She wear her long hair pulled back off her bronze-coloured face and tied at the back of her neck with a red bandana, the same kind Grover wear around his forehead. Her back is straight, her legs long, and she wear a wide black belt on her blue jeans with a single red stone in the silver buckle. Her breasts be high and the silky material of her shirts show them off. She got eyes that don't miss a single thing go on around her.

Finally, after almost two years, some Frenchman from Ottawa, issue a statement saying the charges that the RCMP used false information to "get" Grover Manybears is ridiculous. The new trial is denied, and them guys from Ottawa won't even talk about, let alone agree to meet with Anna Wolverine. "There is simply no new evidence," they say. "We would just be going through everything that was presented the first time around. Manybears' sympathizers are far too eager to believe his claims. Everyone likes a story where the RCMP are the bad guys. No one seems to care about what the RCMP has to say. And what about the two dead constables? Who will speak for them?"

When that announcement come out, Sandra Burn is right here on the Ermineskin Reserve raising money for lawyers, getting signatures on petitions, selling bumper stickers. Grover, he is now at the prison down near Drumheller in the badlands.

"Grover was pretty smart. He looked ahead. He always knew he might get taken," Sandra say to us.

We got a loose organization, here at Hobbema called the Ermineskin Warrior Society, and Sandra be talking to ten or so of us. She tell us what Grover say: "Not safe to pass on information by mouth around a prison,"

Grover told her. "No matter how careful I whisper to you or one of my lawyers, they got microphones can pick up sounds from a mile away. I can tell my lawyer things in confidence, but he's white and I'm Indian. I'm not sure that I can trust him. I hear the FBI went to one of Leonard Peltier's lawyers and said 'Here's $5000 cash, tell us what he told you.' And that lawyer did.

"One time I checked it out," Grover told her. "I slapped my lawyer on the back as he was leaving and said 'You ain't gonna be seeing me no more, because me and a couple of other guys are *walkin'* on Friday night during the movie.' Well, on Friday there was more activity around the joint that anyone seen in years. About supper time they have a shakedown and claim to find illegal stuff in the cell of one of my friends. They cancel the movie, leave us all in our cells, and have a guard with a gun posted about every fifteen feet in the corridors. Must have cost the Government a few thousand for overtime, as well as however much they had to pay my lawyer to fink."

Then what Sandra show us is the way Grover write letters to her. He say, "Don't pay no attention to the first two paragraphs, or the last two, look in the middle. I try not to write more than six paragraphs to a letter and one of them middle paragraphs have a message in it. The second word of each sentence start with the important letter. Most of the paragraphs won't say anything, but you got to check each one careful."

Then she show us a letter he wrote. It look real ordinary. In it he talk about plain things, like how much he miss Sandra and his friends, what records he been listening to, and what books he been reading, and even what some of them books was about.

"Letters should be boring," Grover always say. "If you rant and yell about how they treating you bad and what you gonna do when you get out, that kind of talk keep the censors awake. But if you write a lot of dull stuff they just skip right over it."

"Sometimes when he was first in jail he used to write real sexy letters to me," Sandra tells us. "There wouldn't be any message in them, he'd just do it to entertain that censor guy. Next time the censor be looking for the sexy parts, not find any, and pass the letter right on through."

Sandra circle the important letters of the alphabet in Grover's letter and sure enough they spell out I LOVE YOU.

"He can tell me lots of secrets that way," she say, and laugh pretty.

And he do tell her lots of secrets, one about every second letter. "Won't be nothing special today," Sandra would say, "this one is all full of sexy talk." Then the next letter would be dull but have a message, or part of a message, like one letter which spell out ESCAPE, or another time SEPT., and still another THIRD, and finally ECONO.

The last one puzzle us until, while Sandra is on a visit to the prison at Drumheller, she see a garbage truck with *Econo Disposal* written on its door.

"We never said one suspicious word to each other," Sandra say and laugh, her brown eyes sparkling. "We even talk about me moving to Drumheller and maybe even getting a job there. Made it sound like we're resigned to Grover being inside for a long time, just in case they were listening."

You don't think we get excited as that third of September get closer, and we get even more excited when Sandra say she going to let us help with the escape. She afraid the police might be watching her every time she leave the reserve. Sandra don't even visit that week. She spend her time in Calgary finding a place where it be safe for Grover to hide.

We are outside the jail on that Tuesday night, September third, just like we supposed to be. We have Louis Coyote's pickup truck with me driving, Frank Fence-post and Robert Coyote and their girlfriends. It was Sandra who decided who should make the trip.

Robert, his girl Bertha Bigcharles, and me, sit in the truck. Frank and Connie is in the truck box, drink 7-Up from cans and dance to some music from Frank's transistor radio what he borrow without asking from the Robinson's Store in Wetaskiwin. We figure if we make a little noise, instead of just looking sneaky, we less likely to get checked over by the police.

At about seven o'clock a big blue garbage truck, say *Econo Disposal Co.* on the door, come rolling out the gate. As it turn the corner at the end of the block we follow it.

"What if there's more than one truck?" says Robert.

"We can only follow one at a time," I say. "We have to trust Grover to give us the right time."

That truck drive about five miles out into the badlands and empty its load in a gully what being used as a garbage dump. We watch from the top of a rise maybe half a mile away. We stay right there on the side of the road until that truck pass us on its way back to town.

We can't see no movement there in the garbage but we drive on down anyway. The dump is silent, the only sounds a few magpies and land gulls quarrelling over bits of food. We walk over to where we saw that truck dump its load.

"There's nobody around for miles," yell Frank turning up the volume on his radio. "Come out, come out, wherever you are."

At that the grapefruit halves and cabbage leaves start to move a bit and the head of Grover Manybears, still wrapped in a red bandana, appears.

"You must be Silas," he says to me, shaking some lettuce off his fingers so he can shake hands.

We take him right to the house in Calgary where Sandra has arranged to hide him. Sandra, she is at a bingo game at Blue Quills Hall where everyone will see her and know she couldn't have helped Grover escape.

But that don't stop the RCMP from having a big

search here on the reserve a couple of days later. A dozen or so police cars come slink onto the reserve at about 4:00 AM when everybody is asleep. They circle all the cabins, then start pounding on doors and have a look at everybody they find in each cabin.

As usual the raid is led by Constable Chretien.

"The only way he could be dumber is if he was bigger," is what Frank Fence-post says about him.

Constable Chretien have a photograph of Grover Manybears, one from a magazine where he is peering through prison bars, his red bandana tied across his forehead, his hair touching the shoulders of his white tee-shirt.

The constable have that photo in his left hand and a flashlight in his right. He peer into the sleepy face of each man he find, then shine the light onto the photograph, then back to the suspect Indian as he compare the two.

Sometimes he even take his right hand and cover the forehead of his suspect as he try to imagine that Indian wearing a red bandana.

I wasn't there to see it, but they say Mad Etta tied a red scarf around her forehead and that Constable Chretien spent about half and hour just walking around Mad Etta, staring at her from different angles, trying to decide if he got his man or not.

Now that we got Grover out of jail the big problem is what to do with him. We can move him around Calgary every few days, maybe eventually get him to an Indian reserve somewhere, but it look like he gonna have to hide out for one long time.

"I want to do something with my life. Hiding in someone's spare room ain't that different from prison," Grover say. "And I want to be with Sandra too."

They ain't seen each other since Grover broke out because the police follow every move that Sandra make, which is why she been moving around Edmonton a lot, trying, but not too hard, to lose the police who follow her.

One day, after visiting Grover, me and my friend Frank Fence-post was walking down one of the main streets in Calgary when all of a sudden we run right into my white brother-in-law, Robert McGregor McVey. He come strutting out of one of them tall buildings what is covered in blue glass the colour of moonlight, walk across the sidewalk and right into us. We would of ducked him if we could. Robert McVey is married to my sister Illianna. He don't know how to act around Indians, and just having him around us is kind of like sloshing gasoline on a fire to try to put it out.

Brother Bob is wearing a suit; in fact Brother Bob look like he was born wearing a suit. I can picture him in his crib wearing a little suit and hat, a tie, and shiny shoes with toe rubbers. Today he is carrying a black briefcase that I bet is worth more than everything me and Frank is wearing.

He brush off the front of his suit like maybe he got dirty by bumping into us.

"Well, Silas," he say at me, "it's good to see you."

He says this to me as if I am an RCMP just pulled him over for going a hundred miles an hour.

"Hi there, Brother Bob," I say. We look kind of uneasy at each other. "You remember my friend Frank?"

"I ought to," says Brother Bob, straightening his hat. "He's done more to ruin my life than anyone, except maybe you."

"Hi there, Firechief," says Frank, calling Brother Bob by the Indian name we give him along time ago, and kind of waving his fingers at him and smiling a big, shit-eating smile.

I have to admit we have caused Brother Bob a certain amount of trouble in the past. But we always had good intentions.

Brother Bob look at Frank like he was something a dog left on the sidewalk, and I figure he's about to go on his way, when, just to make conversation, I ask a question that eventually change the lives of quite a few people.

"How is that building you doing in your basement coming along?"

Illianna in one of her letters tell how her and Brother Bob is building a suite in their basement, going to rent it out to make some extra money. I wrote back to say Ignace Monoose, his 17 kids, four dogs, and a pony would be happy to rent it. I point out to Illianna that that way she never get lonesome for the reserve.

Illianna she know I am only joking, but I bet Brother Bob is the kind of guy who reads her mail.

"We're having a little trouble right now," Brother Bob say. "In fact I'm having a lot of trouble hanging the doors."

"Government hanged my grandfather along with Louis Riel," says Frank, as he try to play leapfrog with a parking meter.

"Really?" say Brother Bob.

"Yeah," says Frank. "That was before he got himself a family. If he died that young I never been able to figure how he go to be my grandfather."

"That doesn't make sense," says Brother Bob.

"All I know is when I was little Grandpa Fence-post used to say 'Frank, when I was young I spent a lot of time hanging around with Louis Riel!'"

Brother Bob make a bad face.

By this time I got an idea boiling up like steam in the back of my head.

"Brother Bob," I say, "me and Frank we been to the Tech School at Wetaskiwin; I bet we could hang those doors for you."

"Thanks anyway, Silas, but there's a lot more than doors involved. Actually about all we've done is put up the studs and lay down some flooring. I had a fellow come in and do the wiring, but hiring help is real expensive."

"Brother Bob," I almost yell. "You know what we do

when somebody build a new place on the reserve? Everybody pitch in and do what they is best at. If you got the materials we could finish up that place in no time."

"Oh, I don't think so."

"We work for free." Brother Bob be pretty cheap and I'm counting on that word *free* sinking in. "Besides," I say, "it's the neighbourly thing to do. You're family and all, and we really do owe you a good turn."

Brother Bob protest a lot but the protests get weaker and weaker when he think of all the free work he going to get done.

"Tomorrow's Friday, I'll bring a whole crew down and we get that job finished in no time. No booze. We all be really serious about making up to you for the accidents we've had. Hey, I'll even leave Post-hole here at home if he worry you too much."

Then I drag Frank away by the arm leave Brother Bob stand and hug his briefcase to him like it was a big tomcat.

"You wouldn't really leave me at home would you?" say Frank as we get into the truck.

"I would if I have to," I say. "But right now we got to get to Hobbema and on to Edmonton to find Sandra Burn."

Sandra think my idea is a good one.

"Your brother-in-law's house is in a real fancy district. Police will never look there for Grover."

"There's more to my idea than just moving Grover in there," I say. "I already checked with Mad Etta and she agree with me. We going to move you in there with Grover."

"Oh, no, the police follow me."

"Not the way we got figured."

Then we tell her the rest of my idea.

Next night a whole crew of us arrive at Brother Bob's. He own a fancy house way up in the northwest of Calgary where his back door look out on the foothills. On the way down we sort of acquired a table-saw that sit big in the back of the truck, and Frank and Eathen ripped-off enough tools to start a carpenter shop, from stores in Wetaskiwin, Ponoka, Red Deer, and Airdrie. We bring along Fred Duhamel, who be a real carpenter, Charlie Big Six, who had a year as a plumber's helper, and Billy Bigcharles, who used to work at a sash and door factory.

There was no fooling around. Brother Bob couldn't believe it. By Sunday afternoon we got the walls up and the carpet down, the plumbing installed, and all the paint and wallpaper done just the way it supposed to be.

"This place is all ready to move into," we say.

Brother Bob is some pleased. He run around wringing his hands together and smiling wider than I ever seen before.

"Maybe I could help you to write up an ad for the newspaper," I say, hoping the idea will look like a worm in front of a fish. Brother Bob is feeling so good he accept my offer and him and me sit down at the dining room table and figure out what we want to say.

What we finally come up with is:

> One bedroom basement suite
> for quiet married couple.
> No children. No pets. No
> loud music. 288-5902.

"I know how busy you are Brother Bob," I say, already stuffing the ad in the pocket of my jean jacket. "I'll take this here ad to the newspaper first thing in the morning. Me and Frank will even pay for it. Kind of a suite-warming present..."

"I appreciate that," Brother Bob say. "You know I think you really have turned over a new leaf, Silas."

Brother Bob thank us about ten times for building the suite for him. He even offer us some food. So far we kept Connie Bigcharles running down to the nearest Mac-donald's and 7-11 Stores. "Sorry I don't have any Indian food for you. I should have had Illianna bake some hammock for you."

"Bannock," say Frank.

"Whatever," says Brother Bob.

Boy, we sure move fast when we leave Brother Bob's. The big thing was for me to get away from there with that ad in my pocket. It never gonna get near the newspaper. We've told Grover our plan and he thinks it is a good one. Sandra's not so sure, but she is waiting at Hobbema for us not quite believing that we going to pull it off.

What we said to Sandra the other day was: "What kind of people do the police bother the least?"

"I don't know," she say kind of annoyed. "Ministers or old people..."

"They never bother the kind of Indians come from India," we say, jumping up and down some. "Those kind of Indians are clean, polite, and never cause nobody trouble."

"Just suppose somebody hold up a 7-11 Store," says Frank Fence-post, "then run away and the police come searching for them. If they seen two real Indians on the street the police would run us in for questioning, but if there was two Pakistani Indians on the street, police ask them if they seen anybody around who look suspicious."

"And they'd say they seen *us*," laugh Robert Coyote.

"We going to turn you and Grover into Indian Indians," we say. "You be able to live right under the noses of the police forever."

"Even get jobs," says Frank.

"Well I don't know," says Sandra, but the idea grow on her as she come to see it as a way for her and Grover to be together.

It sure is a surprise the effect clothes has on a person. My girlfriend Sadie One-wound gone shopping in Edmonton on Saturday and bought a couple of these silky dresses that East Indian ladies wear. Bedelia Coyote and Sadie dress Sandra in a sari and sandals, and tie a silky scarf over her head. With some Super Glue they stick a tiny red stone, used to be part of one of Sadie's earrings to Sandra's forehead, just above her nose. When they finish, Sandra who always look as if she just been in a rodeo contest, look soft, silky, and as if she never been near a reserve in her life.

Monday morning we drive Sandra, dressed in jeans, cowboy boots, and a denim jacket, up to the Alice Hotel Coffee Shop in Wetaskiwin. We pretty sure we being followed. Sandra go to the washroom carrying a shopping bag. A few minutes later an East Indian lady come out of the washroom and go across the street to catch the southbound bus for Calgary. The rest of us head off to Calgary too.

Frank stayed in Calgary and Monday morning he rip-off a suit for Grover. Frank just go to a department store, try on a suit one size too large for him. When he come out of the changing room he leap over a counter, run full speed and yell like he being chased by a swarm of bees. "Funny how people get out of your way when you act like that," he say.

Earlier me and Robert Coyote went for a ride in a taxi driven by an East Indian man with a turban. "Hey, partner," we say, "can you take us to a store where they sell turbans like you wearing?" That guy sure look at us funny but he do what we ask. After we get one we say, "We give a $5 tip if you teach us how to tie this here turban up the way you wear yours." He really eye us funny, but everybody like to get five dollars and he do like we ask.

At the place where Grover is hiding we go through the phone book to find new names for him and Sandra. The man who drove the taxi was named Singh, and from the number in the phone book, Singh to Indian Indians must be kind of like Smith to Canadians. There is a big variety of first names: Ajit, Baburam, Charanjit, Dalwir.

Grover settle on Gurdave as a first name, until I point up that it is not much different from Grover. I read in a magazine once that when people take on fake names they often pick the same initials as they had originally. I make sure Grover don't do that. He finally decide his name will be Sanjit Singh, and Sandra will become Ravinder Singh.

We tie that bright scarlet turban around Grover-Sanjit's head and shave his moustache. With him dressed in a grey suit, a vest and tie, and shiny shoes no one would ever know he used to be Grover Manybears.

When Sandra arrives, her and Grover hardly know one another, and don't know whether to touch or not. They shake their heads, laugh, but they keep staring and staring at each other.

"One time at a sawmill I worked with some East Indian guys," Sanjit say. "This idea might just be okay."

Next Grover phone Brother Bob's house. We know Illianna will answer.

"I have seen your kind notice in the newspaper. Please to tell me if the quiet one bedroom is yet rented?" Grover say. I guess she says no, 'cause he go right on. "I am a very quiet couple, please. No children. No pets. And we do not wear our shoes indoors." He makes arrangements to see the rooms after supper.

We haven't told Illianna what we are doing. I know she'd understand, but she been living with a white man for a long time now....

We make sure we are there when Sanjit and Ravinder Singh come to look at the apartment.

Brother Bob's eyes sure get big when he see the way they is dressed. They look at the rooms, say they'll take it right away. "Well we haven't made up our minds," Brother Bob say. "We have to think about it."

"How many other calls you had from the ad I put in?" I say.

"Well, none yet," say Brother Bob.

"I think you'd be just fine," says Illianna. I'm not sure and I probably never will be, but I think when they introduce themselves Illianna sort of flash her eyes across Grover and Sandra's, and I think she sense something. I sure hope she did anyway.

"Not to worry, we will make the place clean for you," Sanjit say, smile like he just took first prize in something.

"It *is* clean," says Brother Bob, in a kind of offended voice.

"Not to feel badly, please. We will make the rooms, how you say it? So clean one could eat off the floor."

"You're not gonna cook with any of that funny stuff, you know…"

"Curry," whispers Illianna.

"Yeah curry or things that will smell the house up."

"Oh, not to worry, please. We are Canadians now. We have learned to cook with bacon grease and cabbage like everyone else."

We keep a pretty close watch on the new tenants for the first few weeks. All our Calgary friends donate furniture, a chair here, a mattress there, an alarm clock from another place. And the people from CIFF send some money.

"I've applied for a government job," Sanjit tell us. "Told them I have three degrees from schools in India. They'll never check them out. I've got an honest face," he say and laugh. "I might even get to work in the Attorney General's Department, wouldn't that be something?"

The next Saturday we is all sitting around in Brother Bob's living room drinking coffee when the doorbell ring. My stomach drop about a foot when I pull back the drapes and see two big Calgary policemen standing on the doorstep.

Illianna is already on her way to the front hall.

I try to keep my voice calm.

"Maybe you should answer it, Brother Bob," I say. "It's the police." Brother Bob jump from his chair like there was a spring under his buns, and bound across the room.

Grover and Sandra move real quick, head off through the kitchen for the basement, take their coffee cups with them.

I can't hear what's being said at the door but it sound pretty businesslike. I take one more peek through he drapes and there is an RCMP car cruising to a stop across the street. And there is another City Police car parked next to our truck. I bet if I was to look out the kitchen window there'd be police cars in the alley too.

Grover-Sanjit told me he took off a piece of wallboard near the furnace and that he got two rifles and enough bullets to last a month hid in there. Neither him nor Sandra plan to get captured without a fight.

"We're looking for the driver of that truck," one of the cops say. "The old Ford."

"Oh, well, in that case," says my brother-in-law, "come on in. The man you're looking for is in the living room."

"The truck is registered to one Louis Coyote," say another voice at the door. For some reason he pronounce Louis' name Ki-o-tee. "Is Mr. Ki-o-tee here?"

"No, sir," I say, walking into the hall. "I'm Silas Ermineskin. Mr. Coyote lets me drive his truck. I have all the papers here," and I haul out my driver's license and Louis' truck registration and insurance card. That policeman look them all over real careful.

"Umph," he finally say and hand them back to me. Then he question me for about ten minutes about where me and the truck was the night Grover Manybears escaped. I explain that the truck was laid up at Fred Crier's Texaco Garage at Hobbema on that day. We already arranged for Fred to back that up.

"And who are all these other people?" ask the police.

Everybody explain who they are.

Police ain't very interested in Frank, Sadie, or Connie. The one they are interested in is Illianna.

"Who did you say you were again?" one constable say to her.

"I'm Illianna McVey, I live here."

"Do all these people live here?" they say to Brother Bob.

"Just me, my wife and son," he say back. "The others are my wife's relatives. At least the one you were questioning is," and Brother Bob look at me like I'm a toilet that just overflowed.

"Do you mind if we have a look around?" say the police.

"Of course not, I have nothing to hide," says Brother Bob. "What is it you're looking for?"

"We're looking for some escaped fugitives…"

I'm pretty sure I can hear Grover in the basement ripping off the wallboard as we are walking around.

Brother Bob laugh. "You won't find any here. I can vouch for Silas and his friend Post-hole over there. They haven't escaped from anywhere, though sometimes I think they should be locked up," and Brother Bob laugh as he ease open the door to Bobby's room. "My son's asleep in there," he say.

The constable look with one eye through the crack in the door.

"Sorry to bother you folks," he says. "We had a report of a truck matching the description of the one outside, seen near the prison the night Grover Manybears escaped. There were Indians in it. And when someone complained that some Indians had parked an old truck so one wheel was on their lawn, here in this respectable district, we thought we'd better check it out."

"That's okay," Brother Bob says, as the constable is half-heartedly opening the door to the linen closet.

"What about downstairs?" says the other officer.

"There's a suite; an East Indian couple live down there."

That constable is poised at the top of the basement

stairs, one foot in open space. I imagine I hear Grover and Sandra cocking their rifles.

"Their names are Rachet and Bravinder Ravinder, or something funny," says Brother Bob.

"Sanjit and Ravinder Singh," says Illianna.

"He wears about two miles of turban around his head and says 'Not to rip my face off, please,'" laughs Frank, who has been following us.

"He works as a speed bump at a parking lot downtown," I say.

"Bet I could arrange for them to work for you," says Frank. "They'd make a nice pair of his-and-hers mud flaps for your cruiser."

"Enough curry down there to singe your nose off," says Illianna, and her eyes flash across mine like raindrops cutting through the glare of a streetlight.

"I don't think we need to bother them," says the first constable, and turn back into the kitchen. "I'm surprised you're all so prejudiced," he add. "East Indian people are our most law abiding citizens."

"Who's prejudiced?" says Brother Bob.

After the police are gone Brother Bob say to me. "Silas, you're a pretty smart fellow. If you know anything about these fugitives, I trust you to do the right thing."

"Oh, you bet, Brother Bob," I say. "You can always trust me to do the right thing."